Riding the danger trail

Lark rode at a canter, into the jaws of Dead Man's Canyon. He had gone two miles . . . three . . . he rounded a sharp bend.

In men like Justin Lark, an instinct builds up. He caught the momentary shine of metal behind a bush. A shot rang out, echoed. Then another bullet struck rock behind Lark as he lunged for cover.

Now it was his move . . .

Stoneman's Gap

a novel by

Robert McCaig

BALLANTINE BOOKS • NEW YORK

Library of Congress Catalog Card Number: 75-35972

ISBN 0-345-24883-X-125

First Edition: February, 1976

Manufactured in the United States of America

BALLANTINE BOOKS
A Division of Random House, Inc.
201 East 50th Street, New York, N.Y. 10022
Simultaneously published by
Ballantine Books of Canada, Ltd., Toronto, Canada

Stoneman's Gap

". . . he is shrewd enough to detect many difficulties before they arise, courageous enough to meet them when they do come, and cool and skilful enough to give them better than they send when the emergency arises."

Hands Up
Gen. David J. Cook
(1840–1907)

1

<<<<<<<<<<<<<<<<<<<<<<<<<<<<<<<<<

Halfway through the eighteen-mile gorge that was Dead Man's Canyon, the Redstone River plunged seething into a slot in the mountain wall. Cliffs of solid rock lifted high and menacing above the racing water where it sluiced through the narrow gateway between the sheer cliffs.

In a singular feat of engineering, the roadbuilders

1

had toiled with pick and drill and blasting powder to carve a shelf in solid rock on the south side of the river. Even then the roadway had to climb steeply to top the shoulder of the promontory before it could drop again toward water level as the canyon widened.

Justin Lark looked back from his seat on the box of the big Concord as the stagecoach negotiated the stretch. At the narrowest reach of the slot, the coach plunged into deep, cool shadow, the vertical walls blocking the June sun. From his place between Mulcahy, the driver, and Percy, the shotgun guard, Lark could see in the brilliant sunlight behind them how steeply the road rose, and the surge and power of the river. Not a place for a fearful man, he thought, and guessed that some of the passengers might be panicky at this close threat of danger.

Mulcahy yelled "Hi-yah!" and sent the lash of his whip curling over the ears of the lead team with a crack like a pistol shot. With a final effort the six horses took the heavy coach over the top of the rise. The road flattened, widened, and began a gentle descent toward the floor of the canyon. Ahead Lark could see a cove indenting the canyon wall, its sparse soil supporting the greenery of alder and aspen. At the near edge of the trees, the waters of a small creek plunged from the cliffs to spin frothing toward the Redstone. A bridge of rough timber spanned the creek. The stage rumbled across it.

From the hillside above the timber, sudden flame lanced down. At Lark's side the shotgun guard, Percy, grunted. His double-barreled shotgun slipped from his grasp and fell to the roadway. As the man sagged sideways, Lark reached out and grabbed him, held him. As he lowered the guard's body to the box, the flaccid inertness of the flesh told Lark that the man was dead.

"Goddamn!" Mulcahy growled. He braced his foot on the brake and hauled the six horses to a stop. He took a twist of the reins around the whip socket and set the brakes. The horses stood quiet, flanks heaving, a light sheen of sweat on their hides. Their ears flicked as the sound of the shot echoed from cliff to cliff.

2

Lark sensed rather than saw heads pop out of the open windows of the coach. Again from the hillside, powder smoke bloomed; a bullet clipped a rock and sang off into the void. From the corner of his eye Lark saw the heads pop back ludicrously, like the action of an animated toy.

Mulcahy muttered, "Road agents, Lark. Don't make no sudden moves. Same damn bunch of Redtops—killers. Oh hell, why did they shoot Percy? No damn need of it. Don't you cross 'em, Lark."

Now a tall, lean man stepped out of the brush at the side of the road. From the opposite side came a short, stocky man. Both held revolvers. With deliberate care Lark inventoried them—nondescript work clothes, battered hats, worn boots. They were masked —not with the makeshift handkerchief over mouth and nose, but with a knitted red covering which hid their faces completely except for an opening for the eyes. They came toward the stage with a businesslike air, cautious enough, but without fear.

Here's a break, Lark thought, if I can come through this alive. He was not afraid, but as always when he was in a tight spot, his heart was pounding with excitement. He forced into the back of his mind the swell of his anger at the wanton murder of the guard, and concentrated on the two men, trying to etch into memory every nuance of voice or action.

The lean man motioned with his gun. "Get down," he said. Mulcahy put foot to step and dropped stiffly to the roadway. Lark, keeping his hands clear of his body, followed him. They stood with their backs against the front wheel of the Concord.

"What about him?" the stocky bandit said, motioning toward the still body on the box, an arm dangling limply over the edge.

"He's dead," Mulcahy said.

The tall man laughed. "Percy, wasn't it? The one that gunned down Tom Towe a while back? Now y'see, old-timer, what happens to any son-of-a-bitch that gets in the way of us Redtops. All right, all right, get them passengers out. Line 'em up."

Lark, standing relaxed against the wheel, heard the crunch of rock chips from behind the coach. He

3

turned his head slowly, to see two more men come from the rear. They had evidently been posted back toward the bridge. They were masked in the same manner. One, slim and young-looking, carried a rifle. The second man was big and blocky, and oddly wore gloves in spite of the heat. Lark placed these two against his mental measuring board as he had the others. Later he would be able to call their heights within a half-inch, their weights within two or three pounds.

"All right, all of you inside, get out here," the lean bandit ordered. "Follow orders, don't get smart, and you won't get hurt. And don't go hidin' anything. That's the kind of foolishness that gets a body killed."

The slim bandit swung the door open, and the passengers stepped down one at a time. Five quite ordinary people, Lark thought—a drummer, a couple of miners, a rancher, and a woman who in her slightly draggled finery would be what was euphemistically called an "actress." They stood nervously, reacting to the situation with various degrees of fear or apprehension.

"Go through 'em, John Doe, and don't miss nothin'," the leader ordered. The gloved robber held his gun on the passengers from one side, the chubby man on the other, and the slight bandit, putting his rifle down, shook out a cloth sack. He began collecting wallets, watches, rings, and loose change. The take looked slim. Lark guessed that these experienced travelers had known the hazards of Dead Man's Canyon, and disposed their valuables accordingly. The collector grabbed Lark's wallet and flipped it open. He cursed when he found less than twenty dollars, and hurled the leather to the ground and kicked it with a scarred boot. "Dam' cheapskate!" he grumbled.

He took a small roll of bills from the reticule of the woman as she watched, her face set and angry. Then he grabbed her hand and twisted a flashy ring from her finger. She cried out, "You hurt me, damn you! It's only paste, anyhow."

"My girl won't know the difference," the man said. Then, stooping, he lifted the hem of her skirt high and ran a hand over her bare shapely thighs. "Like I thought, a nice deposit in the lisle-thread

4

bank," he said, grinning. He ripped a sizable wad of bills from beneath her clothing and let the skirt drop.

She spat square in his face. His hand flashed out in a backhand blow, and a ring on the hand ripped her cheek from ear to chin. She staggered back against the coach and clapped her handkerchief to the seeping wound, muttering obscenities not quite loud enough for the man to make out.

The tall man laughed. "You'll learn, sister. You'll learn like the rest of 'em," he said. "You, driver—Mulcahy, ain't it?—come on back here and open the boot."

From his position, Lark could not see what was taking place at the back of the coach, and he did not consider it expedient to take a single step for a better view. Though the slight bandit was in the coach, searching for any possible hidden articles, two others still stood, guns in hand, not to be challenged. Moreover, there was still the threat of the hidden rifleman on the slope ahead, the man who had killed Percy. So Lark stood quiet, listening for any word, any phrase, of telltale speech.

He heard a rip of knife through canvas, and Mulcahy's protest, "But mister, that's the United States mail!"

The tall bandit laughed again. "Who the hell cares? Hey, here's what I'm looking for! 'Bear Consolidated Mining Company, Magma, M.T.'" There was a tearing sound and a hoarse shout. "Hey, boys, look here! All these purty pieces of paper—ain't they something?"

"Man, oh man, that's the jackpot, Ra—" the gloved man exclaimed, greed dripping from his voice. He had started to add a name.

"Shut up, you jackass!" the leader snapped. "Come on, let's get out of here. John Doe and Richard Roe, you bring up the horses."

"Ain't we gonna go through the baggage?" the chubby man asked.

"Hell with it, time's too short. We got what we come after. Doe, you signal for Smith to come down now. These folks ain't about to give us any trouble, are you, folks?"

5

Only the woman answered. "You filthy swine will get yours, just you wait and see. The nerve, feeling up a lady's legs like that! Bunch of damn perverts."

"Madam, keep talking and you'll get the other side of your face busted. So shut up," the tall man said. "Now, Mulcahy, you stay right here for fifteen minutes." He chuckled. "Oh hell, I forgot you ain't got a watch anymore. Well, judge it by the sun, and make it generous. We been knowed to wait around a bend with a little surprise for people that don't follow orders. You get me, pal?" His voice was harsh with threat.

"I get you, mister," Mulcahy said, quietly enough, though Lark could almost hear the grinding of the driver's teeth.

The leader started to turn away, toward the spot ahead where his men were waiting with the horses. He said, "Well, thank you, folks, for your contributions. Don't forget to show your friends that dead meat up on the box—remind 'em what happens to anyone who gets in the way of the Redtops. And don't you forget the lesson, either."

Lark watched them mount and spur their horses west. As they reached the bend, another mounted man joined them—the marksman from the hillside, Lark decided. That man was not masked, but he was so far away that the fleeting glimpse was not enough to identify any characteristics.

With the gunmen gone, the passengers broke into excited talk, about what they should have done, what Mulcahy should have done, who the bandits might be, why the Robbins and Tucker Stage Lines didn't protect passengers against such terrible treatment.

Mulcahy gave them short shrift. "All right, all right, get back in the coach. You gotta remember that by God's grace you're still alive. Pore Percy is dead. That was part of the Redtop gang and they've killed half a dozen men or more. So you count your blessings while we head for the Gap."

As the passengers, still grumbling, began to climb back into the Concord, Lark walked back along the road. He found Percy's shotgun, scratched but not

6

damaged, where it had fallen. He picked it up and carried it back to the coach, where Mulcahy was stuffing the scattered letters back into the slashed mail pouch.

"How much d'you think they got?" Lark asked the driver.

"Dunno. Ten thousand, maybe," Mulcahy said, buckling the straps over the boot. "The package and a coupla hundred from the passengers. Most times the Magma package would have been in the strongbox, but this gang takes box and all, so I guess the Bear people thought they'd get cute and send it through reg'lar mail, not even registered. Redtops knew it, though. They must have a wire into the post office."

"Or the Bear Consolidated office, or the bank that supplied the bills for the payroll, which I suppose the shipment was," Lark said. He and Mulcahy climbed to the box and laid the body of the guard on the coach roof, securing it to the baggage rail.

Mulcahy sat back in the driver's seat. He dusted his hands and seized the reins. "Them bastards ought to be long gone by now," he said. "Guess it's safe to head for the Gap."

The rested horses took the big Concord down the road at a handsome clip. As the stage rocked and jolted along the uneven roadway, Lark asked, "Where does this Redtop gang hang out?"

"God only knows. As many jobs as they've pulled, every time they just fade into thin air afterwards. 'Course, some folks have their suspicions, but they don't mention 'em, not very loud, leastwise. Y'see, Lark, the law in Antelope County . . ." He stopped, giving Lark a wary look. He chuckled without mirth. "There I go, shootin' off my mouth about something I don't know a damn thing about. Lark, I gotta drive this rig through Dead Man's Canyon three, four times a week. And I pass a dozen dry gulches between Fort Ruskin and Mantoul. So I do my best to keep my big mouth shut at all times. You seen what happened to pore Percy."

Lark nodded. I'll hear it all in good time, he thought. No point in pushing too hard. Sure a break to have

7

been on a stage the Redtops held up, to have seen exactly how they work. What a story this will make! And what a bunch of characters to add to Aunt Susan's collection!

2

Stoneman's Gap, M.T.
June 26, 1887

Dear Aunt Susan:

My stage was held up by a gang the locals call the Redtops. The guard, a man named Percy, was murdered. They took the money of all the passengers (including me), also a payroll destined for the Bear Mines at Magma. It was mailed in Mantoul; the thieves knew about it, went right to it. Somebody in P.O., or bank? Or Bear Consol. office?

Miss Rimi Woodford, who operates Stoneman's Inn and is postmistress, has employed me on a temporary basis. Will write more tomorrow. No, I did not get hurt in holdup, am in fine fettle. Hope you are the same.

Your aff. nephew,
Justin

<<<<<<<<<<<<<<<<<<<<<<<<<<<<<<<<<<<<

An hour later, with a final crack of the whip, Mulcahy brought his six weary horses and the heavy Concord around the driveway at Stoneman's, to stop in front of the inn with some semblance of a flourish. Lark reached behind him for his canvas-cased guitar, thankful that the Redtop gang hadn't been curious about it. He put a foot on the iron step and jumped to the ground. The guitar made a little thrum of protest as his heels hit the hard gravel. He waited while the driver fastened the reins and climbed down, then went with Mulcahy to the rear boot and helped him unload the baggage. A youth of about sixteen came down the porch steps and picked up part of it, and Mulcahy went inside with the boy, carrying the rest of it.

Lark paused with his foot on the bottom step. Here I go again, he thought. Before those wild cucumber vines have grown enough to shade this porch, it will be all over. I'll be gone or I'll be dead. This is the way I feel at every assignment, the way I felt at Cobo Wells, and Walkerville, and Genesee Flats. The pattern is the same: dig into the lives of people I've never known, the very digging to change subtly or violently the tenor of their lives, even to change their fate. I'll hobnob and carouse and pretend friendship with men I despise. And hour by hour, day by day, I'll lay my life on the line. So far, Justin, you've been lucky, but some day your mother wit, your speed of hand and eye, will fail you. Then—well, this frontier land shows a man small mercy. It's reckless, uncaring, even insane.

Knowing this, why am I here again? The lives I needed to avenge were avenged long since. I collected payment and overpayment for those bills. But one day soon in these Antelope Flats, or the Padlock Valley or the soaring peaks of the Running Wolfs, I'll have to present another bill, nor stay my hand until I can mark the account PAID IN FULL. I swore at Genesee Flats that was the last time, but now I mean it. I'll mail my last letter to Aunt Susan, wipe the blood from my last paycheck and cash it, and buy into some peaceful business. Like this posthouse, maybe—imagine Justin Lark, the smiling boniface, presiding in his inn, meeting the world, his only worry an occasional drunk or deadbeat, or the late arrival of the Mantoul coach.

Lark shook his head at the wryness of his thoughts, and went up the wide steps. He shifted his guitar case and duffel bag and entered the front door. The lobby was large, clean and well-lighted. On the right, double doors opened into a spacious dining room.

Straight back, a door bore the discreet sign TAP ROOM. Beyond the dining room, a hall led to a wide curving staircase, beyond which were other doors.

To his left, Lark saw double French doors opening into a bright airy room, which would be what was generally called the Ladies' Parlor. Near the doors, a counter blocked a corner of the lobby, with a rack of pigeonholes behind it. Another neatly lettered sign read POST OFFICE.

At the lobby desk, the last of the passengers clinked his tagged key and followed the youngster with his baggage toward the hall and the staircase. Lark crossed the lobby and said to the pretty girl behind the counter, "Supper and a bed for the night, ma'am."

She looked at him, frowning, her clear blue eyes distraught. Her light bright hair was disheveled, and there was a spot of ink on her smooth cheek. She turned the registration book toward him and said, "You're from the stage? Then that will be fifty cents for the meal and a dollar and a quarter for your room. Though I don't suppose you have any money, after what happened."

"To be truthful, I am low in funds, but not entirely because I was robbed," Lark said, smiling. "I was hoping for something cheaper in the lodging line—a bunkhouse, perhaps?"

"Why, yes, we have one down at the wagon yard, across the road," she said, studying his signature, *Justin P. Lark,* on the register. "Rather Spartan accommodations, but clean. We charge two bits a night for them."

"Good enough. Take the six bits out of this, ma'am, my only double eagle. I had it in my boot, luckily. I'll be around here for a few days—at least as long as that golden boy lasts. It behooves me to stretch my little poke like a gutta-percha band until I hook up with some work."

She looked at him, back at the signature, then at Lark again, her lower lip caught between white teeth. Then she said, "Mr. Lark, you are looking for work? Can you handle a four-horse hitch? You can? Then I've got a job for you tomorrow, if you'll take it. Maybe

10

you wouldn't want it after what happened today, but it's just for the one time, I think.'"

"A job's a job, when a man's on his uppers," Lark said cheerfully. "What can I do for you?"

"I have the posthouse contract with the Robbins and Tucker Stages, and it includes a shuttle run from here to Magma, twenty-four miles south. Since there isn't enough traffic for a regular coach, we use a mud wagon with a four-horse hitch. Passengers for Magma spend the night here at the inn, and take the shuttle in the morning. Then the stage wagon comes back in the afternoon with the Magma departures. I have a man, a hostler, who drives the shuttle stage, but I have word he's sick in Magma with some kind of miseries. One of the boys from XL handled the run today, but I need a driver for tomorrow."

"You get the customers coming and going, eh?" Lark asked. "I'm your man, then, Miss—Miss . . ."

"Woodford, Rimi Woodford," she supplied. "Then in the morning, Mr. Lark, I'd appreciate it if you'd give Mulcahy a hand getting his teams harnessed and getting the coach out—he'll be leaving for Fort Ruskin at dawn. With Clyde gone, my young brother Phil has so many duties the kid is bushed. We're always shorthanded, it seems."

"I had it in mind to help Mulcahy anyhow," Lark said. "Miss Woodford, we'll need a piece of old canvas, say about eight by ten, and some bits of rope."

"To wrap . . . ?" she asked tentatively.

Lark nodded. "Mulcahy wants to take Percy's body in to Fort Ruskin. He'll turn it over to the law there."

"Law!" she said tersely. "The law means Pete Looby, the high sheriff of Antelope County. And his law is a joke. You saw an example this afternoon, Mr. Lark. Robbery with impunity, wanton murder of a good man. Don't tell me about the law."

"It sure must be disturbing, ma'am," Lark said in a placating tone. "You depend on your customers, and to have them threatened or robbed or killed—well, it's bad for business, if nothing else. You seem to have a good operation here, too, barring this cloud of evil which seems to be hanging over your valley."

"Our location is ideal—this is the crossroads of the

11

whole northwest quarter of the Territory. My inn is needed, by the Robbins and Tucker Stages, by the freighters, by the ranchers. And there's the chance that this place might—well, become even more important. But this evil you mention, and evil it is, threatens to destroy me and the whole region. My own father and uncle—oh, Mr. Lark, I can't burden you with all my worries. You go ahead to the bunkhouse. You'll find that canvas you need in the loft of the barn; I'm sure there's a piece big enough for that sad purpose."

"We'll find it, and thanks, Miss Woodford," Lark said. He picked up his bag and the guitar case and turned toward the door.

"Supper's in an hour," she said. "Mr. Lark . . ." As he looked back, she nodded at the guitar case. "Maybe when things are more cheerful, you'll favor us with some music."

"I'm just a barnyard plunker and a bathtub baritone," he said, smiling. "But when the right occasion arises, I'll try."

The bunkhouse serving the less affluent itinerants at Stoneman's Gap proved to be clean and comfortable. In fact it was a cut above most inns themselves along these Western roads. Its cubicles were small and furnished only with a cot and a dresser. But the beds were clean, without a sign of vermin. There was no door on the cubicle, but this did not worry Lark. He had little to steal and nothing to conceal. In fact, at this point he would welcome an inspection if there were any interested party at Stoneman's Gap.

Lark found Mulcahy and climbed the ladder into the barn loft while the driver waited below. He brought down the piece of old canvas, and together they wrapped the stiffening body of the murdered man. They roped the bundle securely, and debated briefly where to store the corpse. They decided that the roof of the coach, where Percy would take his last ride tomorrow, would be as good a place as any. They hoisted the considerable weight back onto the roof and secured it to the baggage rail.

"A good man, Percy," Mulcahy said in brief eulogy. "Not scairt of a thing in this world except that woman he lived with. I'd like to see 'em hang the guys that shot him, but they never will."

"The law isn't much force this side of the Running Wolfs, eh?" Lark asked.

"It's a joke, mister, a criminal joke. No man is safe, nor woman, neither, as you've seen for yourself. Them Redtops—but there I go, popping off again. Let's wash up and go to supper."

In his cubicle, Lark stripped to the waist and laid out clean clothes on the cot. At the wooden sink outside, he reveled in volumes of cold water piped down from the rocks behind the inn. Mulcahy, already more or less clean, watched as Lark finished and shook the excess water from his hands. No doubt the driver observed that Lark's lean appearance was deceptive, that his chest and shoulders were plated with smooth bands of muscle. The white blaze of a scar slashed his left chest from shoulder to nipple. In back, just at the rib line, was a puckered scar dimpled deep enough for a fingertip.

"Takes two sessions to get clean," Mulcahy observed. "The first turns the dust into mud, and the second washes the mud off. It's sure as hell cold, though."

"It is that," Lark said, mopping himself with a towel. "Be with you in a minute, Mulcahy."

Inside, he donned his undershirt, and buckled on the shoulder harness that held the deadly little derringer unobtrusively under his left arm. He patted the gun as he settled it into place. "You damn near had some use today, feller," he whispered. "Like when that little skunk hit the woman. Of course, even if I had nailed him, I'd be a dead man now." He put on his clean flannel shirt and settled it into place over the hidden holster.

Walking up to the inn with Mulcahy, Lark said, "Nice place Miss Woodford has here."

"Yeah, if she can hang onto it," Mulcahy said, knocking a grasshopper off a grass blade with a spurt of tobacco juice. "She keeps a clean place, and serves the best of grub. Honest, it's the best stopping place in all the Territory, as far as I've heard tell. Man's glad to get here westbound; it means he's safe through

13

Dead Man's Canyon. Eastbound, o' course, nobody sleeps very good with the canyon ahead of him."

"I wish I could guess where the thieves went. Like today."

"To the four winds, maybe. Y'see, Lark, that slot in the rock ain't as solid as she looks. Four, five streams cut into 'er from that south side. They lead back into the Running Wolf peaks. Man afoot or a-horseback can sift back along one or another of 'em, if he knows what he's doing, and acourse the Redtops do. The trails are tougher'n hell, and scary, they say, but nobody ain't gonna follow a man with a gun up them cliffs and over them ridges. So they can get clean away easy enough."

"But that would mean a local tie-in," Lark said.

"You didn't hear me say nothin' like that, Lark," Mulcahy said sharply. "In fact, you didn't hear me say nothin'. Come along, let's eat."

Lark found the meal of soup, roast beef, mashed potatoes, and gravy good, and enjoyed something unusual, a salad of new lettuce and watercress. The meal was topped with a generous slab of dried-peach pie. Finished, Lark leaned back feeling that he had gotten more than his four bits' worth. He could see now why the inn enjoyed such good custom, and why the Robbins and Tucker Stages would be pleased with their contract arrangement.

The meal had been efficiently served by a golden-haired girl of about twelve, and a very stout 'breed woman, who barely managed to clear the swinging door into the kitchen. Lark finished his second cup of excellent coffee, and quill toothpick in hand, went out to the lobby. He saw several of the other male passengers disappear into the taproom, but he tossed his toothpick away and sauntered across the lobby. In the ladies' parlor, he found Rimi Woodford sorting the crumpled letters which had been brought in the ripped mail sack.

The girl looked up from her task, frowning. "Mr. Lark, I hope you enjoyed your supper," she said. "About the shuttle—it doesn't leave until nine tomorrow, so you'll have plenty of time to get ready. Four passengers for Magma—three men and the—the lady over there. Phil will give you a hand getting the rig ready."

"Good enough," Lark said. He nodded toward the taproom door. "I see some of my traveling companions managed to preserve some of their funds."

"Most people traveling in this country stash most of their valuables in the safest place they can find," she said. "The holdup men are usually in a hurry, and can't take time for a detailed search. Anyhow they're mostly after what's in the strongbox, or the mail sacks." She flicked a sideward glance at the "actress" sitting at the end of the room and added softly, "Though I understand one bank was robbed rather roughly. I put some peroxide and sticking plaster on the woman's cheek. I don't think she'll have a scar."

"She almost got herself killed," Lark said soberly. "She's got more nerve than sense. Well, good night, Miss Woodford. I think I'll turn in. It's been a tiring day."

"You're wise—our dawn comes very early," she said. "I wish I could follow suit, but there are a thousand things . . . Mr. Lark, I do appreciate you taking that job."

"It's a pleasure. And call me Justin. It sits better."

"Fine, Justin. Then I'll see you in the morning." And for the first time he saw her smile. It illuminated her whole face.

Then, watching her, he saw the smile vanish. She was looking past him, and over her face swept a look of disbelief, and fear, and finally anger. Turning, Lark saw that a man had just come in the front door. He was young, slim, dressed in well-worn clothes not too clean. His hat was a battered felt. He wore a cartridge belt buckled around his waist, with a holstered pistol tied down along his thigh. He stood blinking in the light of the coal-oil lamps. Now he saw Rimi Woodford, and came toward her, his spurs jingling.

The girl lifted the hinged board and stepped from behind the counter. Frowning, she snapped, "Buzz, you turn right around and get yourself out of here! I told you that you aren't welcome at Stoneman's Inn."

"Aw, Rimi, you're just funnin' me, ain't you?" the young man asked, grinning, showing uneven yellowed

15

teeth. "After all the money I spent here last winter?"

"What money?" she asked scornfully. "Buzz, I mean it—you get out of here and don't come back."

"I got money now. And Rimi, girl, I ain't in the habit of bein' told what I can do," the man said, coming a couple steps nearer. "Leastwise not by no girl. I'm gonna go into your taproom and have me a drink."

Lark moved with that effortless smoothness that was his, and stepped in front of the man Buzz. He said in a pleasant voice, "You hear the young lady, cowboy. Better do as she tells you."

"What the hell is your put-in, mister?" Buzz said harshly. "Get out of my way. I'll show this little bitch. . . ."

The man's bullying tone, his braggadocio, touched a nerve in Lark. Violence and brutality and frustration had been thrust upon him this day, and any more of it was suddenly intolerable. Without warning, Lark drove a fist like a stone into the man's belly, as hard as he had hit a man in all his life. Buzz sagged forward, the wind driven out of him. Lark's hand flicked to the man's holster and yanked out the gun. His other hand went to the coat collar and from the neck sheath extracted a hunting knife, a double-edged Arkansas toothpick. With a twist of the wrist, Lark flipped the knife, which turned through the air to chunk into the door jamb and stick deep, quivering.

Buzz came partly erect, his breath returning in painful sucking sounds, a wheezing rasp in his throat. Hugging his middle with both hands, not quite comprehending, he saw Lark shuck the shells from the six-gun, and extract a dozen spares from the cartridge belt. Lark dropped the shells into his pocket and jammed the pistol back into Buzz's holster.

"Any man's a fool to pack a gun as rusty and leaded up as that one," he said, coolly. "You'd do better to keep it empty or leave it at home, or you'll get yourself killed. Now, sonny boy, get out of here."

"I'll git, but I'll be back. I'll take care of you, Rimi, and you too, mister," Buzz gasped. "Next time I see you, you better be wearin iron."

"Oh, can the threats, kid," Lark said wearily. "If you come after me, they'll pack you away in a pine box. I'm telling you just this once—you come back to Stoneman's Inn, you bother Miss Rimi one more time, and I'll kill you like I would a snake."

"You can't threaten me," Buzz blustered.

"I never threaten," Lark said coldly. "I'm just telling you, mister, in plain English, exactly what I intend to do to you if you come here again. I've had more than one hardcase swear to kill me, but none of them are around any more."

Buzz started to splutter something, then, under Lark's steely glance, the man's eyes dropped and he turned away. At the door he yanked at the imbedded knife and finally got it free. He held it a moment, glowering at Lark, then his nerve broke. He wrenched open the door and ran out. The door slammed shut behind him.

"Thank you, Mr. Lark—Justin," Rimi Woodford said. "But I must warn you, you've made an enemy tonight, and a bad one."

"He doesn't worry me," Lark said. "He's the kind of hammerhead I've never had any use for. Who is he?"

"His name is Robert Bailor; everyone calls him Buzz. His family owns a ranch, Box B, a dozen miles to the south of us. They run a few hundred head, but most of their time is spent in brawling, getting in and out of hot water. Any trouble in this part of the Territory is pretty sure to have a Bailor mixed up in it, or a Prettiman, or a Sumter. They're all related."

"Why did this Buzz come here tonight?"

"He soft-soaped me into letting him run up a bar bill last winter and this spring. My hostler, Clyde Prettiman, is a distant relative of his, and Clyde told me how Buzz was bragging about all the money he took me for, and about some other things, things that weren't true, nasty things. So I put the run on Buzz in no uncertain terms. I suppose he thought I'd forgotten by now."

"So these Bailors are often in trouble with the law?"

"That would be a hard thing to do in Antelope County, even for Bailors," she said, bitterness in her voice. "Some say the Bailors might have a connection with the Redtops, and know more than a little about

17

the robberies and holdups. But I'm not so sure of that—they're reckless and crooked, but I don't think they have the brains to have kept from getting caught."

"Damn!" Lark exclaimed, half under his breath.

Rimi Woodford looked at him sharply. He said quickly, "I just thought of something left undone, Miss Rimi, or to do over. As for that hardcase, I should have killed him. And I would have if it didn't get blood all over your nice clean floor."

"Thanks for your consideration," she said dryly.

Lark smiled, lifted a hand in the shadow of a salute, and left the inn.

At the bunkhouse, a quick check showed Lark he was alone. By this hour the sun had sunk below the distant peaks of the Padlock Mountains, though the sky was still stained with sunset glow. Streamers of color drifted in constantly changing patterns over the Antelope Flats, and to the north of them over Padlock Valley. In the east, only the tips of the Running Wolf peaks still flared in the fading light, the bulk of them looming dark and ominous. Standing in the doorway, Lark heard an early coyote yap from a nearby hilltop, to be answered from afar off. Otherwise the Redstone Valley was quiet and peaceful.

In his cubicle, Lark unstrapped and opened the guitar case. He touched a certain diamond in the inlaid wood of the guitar, and a small door popped open. Reaching into the instrument, he took out a small parcel wrapped in oiled silk, and unfolded it. He straightened the sheaf of bills and stuffed them into the battered wallet which had earlier that day been marred by the bandit's boot. Snapping the inlaid section back, he replaced the guitar in its case.

He undressed slowly, mulling over the events of the day. It's a good start, he thought. I muffed a chance by hurrahing young Bailor, but I didn't realize it then. I doubt if I would have done things differently if I had known his connections. There was a gain, too; I'm in solid with the girl Rimi. I'll bet that pretty young lady knows as much about what goes on from Fort Ruskin to Mantoul as any person along the Running Wolfs, and that includes the sheriff. Someday soon she'll talk to me . . . Damn! I hate this nosing into private affairs. But usually it's the only sure approach.

He hung the shoulder holster with its derringer so the vicious little gun was only inches from his fingertips. Then he rolled in, and with the clear conscience of the just man, he was almost instantly asleep.

3

Stoneman's Gap, M.T.
June 27, 1887

Dear Aunt Susan:

My temporary job for the proprietor of Stoneman's Inn, Miss Rimi Woodford, is driving the shuttle stage from the Gap to Magma. I'm getting my feet on the ground. Some interesting characters in this region, by names of Bailor, Prettiman, and Sumter. I wonder about them, where they came from, etc.

I have given up the idea of doing land-looking. My present occupation as driver, hostler, and handyman, looks like it will be more productive. Will not need our friends from Denver for some time yet.

You'd like this country, auntie, it is very fine.

Your aff. nephew,
Justin

≪≪≪≪≪≪≪≪≪≪≪≪≪≪≪≪≪≪≪≪≪≪≪≪

Lark tooled the four-horse hitch around the turnoff five miles west of the Gap, and turned south down the road toward Magma. None of his four Magma passengers had elected to ride the box with him, which pleased him well enough, for he had some thinking to do. He wanted also to become familiar with this

19

branch road—so familiar that he could travel it by day or by night, afoot or on horseback, with absolute surety. More than once, an exact knowledge of the terrain he was operating in had been Justin Lark's margin between success and failure.

This day in early summer was bright, even brilliant with sunshine. The morning air was still cool, but there was a promise of heat for the hours to come. As he urged his horses on toward the little mining city, Lark found that the road wound along a tumbling small creek which burbled its way through willow and alder at the base of rolling foothills, which climbed to his left toward the Running Wolf bastion. West, to his right, a broken flat extended into the distance, its soil almost desert, sagebrush and prickly pear sparsely dotting stretches of gravel and alkali. The poverty of those Antelope Plains was in sharp contrast with the lush grass of the ascending foothills, open parks patterned with groves of pine and fir.

Better now than on his maps, Lark could see how the Running Wolf range split this country in two. The soaring peaks climbed high above timberline, cloud-drenched, jagged pyramids of rock capped with eternal snow. Few passes pierced that barrier, and one of them was Dead Man's Canyon.

Beyond the flats, to the northwest, lay the Padlocks, and the big mining camp of Copperton. Separating the flats from Padlock Valley was a high ridge, the beginning of the fine cattle country along the Redstone. All this had been buffalo country not long ago, Lark knew. He tried to imagine this land black with the endless herds of huge shaggy beasts, the earth shaking to the thunder of their hoofs. Now they were gone, gone to the Sharps of the robe hunters and the deliberate policies of the U.S. Army. Hunt the buffalo to extinction; without his wild cattle the Indian will starve, and the white man can move in. Well, Lark thought cynically, the policy is working, but they might as well have killed off the Indians, too. He had friends among the tribesmen, great and good friends, who with their wives and children were now reduced to abject poverty, subsisting on the reservation handouts of stringy beef and spoiled potatoes. Lark shook

20

his head at the pity of it—the red men had been tough and brutal, and they had killed white men. But this had been their land, and they didn't deserve starvation and degradation because they had fought to keep it.

With an effort, Lark turned his thoughts away from the injustices which were beyond his powers to remedy, to his own situation. Already a pattern was forming, a pattern which went beyond the depredations of a gang of thieves, to something larger, more menacing. In this frontier country, three things were treasured—minerals, water, land. And if the key to this riddle was land, it would center around the strategic position of Stoneman's Gap.

The Gap commanded the eighteen-mile stretch of Dead Man's Canyon, where over the eons the waters of the Redstone had cut a slot between the peaks, to the fertile Starr Valley to the east of the range. A water-level route, along which in earlier days a toll road had been built with tremendous labor and huge expense. Later the road had become a public thoroughfare, though Antelope County did little or nothing to maintain it. The freighters and the Robbins and Tucker Stages grudgingly did whatever maintenance was absolutely necessary to keep the road operable.

Rimi Woodford's father and uncle must have been men of vision, Lark thought, since they had built their inn at a key point on the only road through the range for a hundred miles to the north and seventy miles to the south. Long ago the Army had recognized the strategic location of the Gap, for they had built a fort in the nearby valley and maintained it until some six years ago, when it had been abandoned with the cessation of the Indian wars. Today there was little left of Fort Meloy except a quadrangle marked by old foundations, a decaying watchtower, and a decaying cemetery. The timbers of the abandoned buildings had long since been hauled away by the valley ranchers.

Stoneman's Inn itself had been a surprise to Lark. The standard post stop on the Western stage routes was a low log structure, dark, odorous, an excuse for a man to get in out of rain or cold, and purchase some sort of provender, usually bad. But Stoneman's Inn was a spacious, two-story building, bright with paint and glass, with running water, and wonder of wonders, an indoor bathroom at each end of the upper hall. The inn was clean and free from vermin. Its meals were excellent. To Lark's mind the inn compared well with the fine posthouses on the well-traveled highways of the East. He wondered what had happened to the two Woodfords. Judging by Rimi's hesitant manner, their deaths must have been violent. Perhaps Aunt Susan can find out something about it from her files of the Fort Ruskin newspapers, he thought.

At the top of a rise, Lark guided his horses to the side of the track for a rest. The breather would keep his rig out of the way of the approaching freight wagons. He swung down from the box to adjust a harness strap on one of his horses, and the passengers got out for a stretch. Lark straightened to watch the freight outfit come storming up the slope, the skimmer astride the near wheeler, his jerkline stretched through loops to the bridle of the near lead mule, with the jockey stick connecting to the off leader.

The wagons loaded light, maybe empty, Lark decided, as the twenty mules brought the tandem of three heavy wagons up the hill, with little effort. With bells jingling, trace chains rattling, the outfit rumbled past the halted stage. The skinner raised his whip in salute, but he did not stop to rest his mules, confirming Lark's guess of empty wagons. The tandem topped the ridge and the mules braced their small neat hooves against the descending weight of the three wagons. Brakeblocks squealed on iron tires as the crew set the brakes. A drift of gray dust following them, the wagons dropped down and out of sight into the woods below.

Lark sent the mud wagon at a brisk pace toward Magma. He watched for the turnoff to the Bailor spread. He found it where a smaller creek came down out of the hills to join Pioneer Creek. A dim track led off into the hills, meandering, almost overgrown. Its junction with the main road was marked by a weathered board hanging cattywampus on a tree, its burned-in legend barely discernible—Ⓑ—Block B. From what I've heard of them, I might want to pay them a visit one of these days, Lark thought.

Among thicker timber, through air redolent of pine and fir, the stage went up one roller-coaster ridge and down another. The road broke into the open, and Lark could see the town of Magma. Though Pioneer Creek kept on up its valley, the road turned toward the town along a smaller creek bed. Lark saw that it was almost dry, and what water it held quite gray and dispirited. He learned why when the road rounded the end of a low earthen dam that crossed the flat below the town. The berm impounded a lake of discolored, lifeless water, still and ugly against grassless banks. Lark guessed that there must have been pressure, even violence, when the ranchers below tangled with the mine operators to protect the purity of the water supply of Pioneer Creek. And the ranchers won that dust-up, he thought with a smile. Usually, with mud or slag or tailings, even cyanide, it was "Let 'er rip!"

Now the road climbed crookedly and steeply toward the town. As the stage drew nearer, Lark studied the place with interest. Magma had a reputation for turbulence, and unbraked violence, and here he might find some of the answers he sought.

Magma was jammed tightly into a cove in the mountain, the harsh rock walls towering above the straggling main street. Its buildings could be only a few years old, but they looked as if they had been there for decades. Above the business area, shacks and cabins swarmed over the hills without apparent order, wooden excrescences on ridge and slope, and rusty dugouts topped with corrugated iron. The hills had been denuded of timber, the trees cut for mine stulls and props, or burned for heating, or fed into the maw of the insatiable furnaces of the smelter.

Dominating the town, high on the rear headwall, Lark could see the headframes of two mines, one at each side of the apex of the main street. They were both working, for he could see the great bull wheels at the top of the gallows frames spin, and stop, reverse and spin again. White puffs of exhaust steam

23

from the hoisting engines rose now and again like Indian smoke signals.

Lark drove his rig up the slant of the main street, and spotted on a corner the brick building he was looking for. Its sign read:

ROBBINS & TUCKER
STAGE STATION—FREIGHTING
CONNECTIONS TO ALL THE WEST

He set the brake, climbed down from the box, and pulled open the door of the mud wagon. As his four passengers clambered out, Lark unstrapped the cover of the boot and heaved down their dusty baggage. Without adieus beyond a wave of the hand, the four clumped off along the high wooden sidewalk. The walk was elevated, Lark supposed, to keep pedestrian feet reasonably dry in winter, and when a torrential mountain rain struck the town.

He entered the office and found a man of middle age behind the counter that stretched the width of the room. He was frowning over papers. At the sound of the door the man looked up at Lark from under a green celluloid visor. He dropped the papers and, hitching up the black sateen sleeve protectors he wore, he stared at Lark, his mustache quivering, his eyes warm with an instant dislike for any intruder.

Lark slung the anemic mail sack onto the counter. "Here's the mail from Stoneman's Gap. You want it?"

"Of course I want it. Robbins and Tucker have the mail contract, don't they? And in Magma, *I'm* Robbins and Tucker. Who are you?"

"My name is Lark. Miss Woodford asked me to bring the stage in, since Prettiman turned up sick."

"Sick, is he? Well, Clyde Prettiman ain't sick any more, I can tell you." The manager cackled at his simple wit.

"Then he can take the stage back down to the Gap," Lark said.

The manager cackled again. "Mister, Clyde's last journey will be uphill, not down, until he takes that greased slide to hell. He's dead."

24

"Dead? What happened to him?"

"Magma poisoning. He got drunk, went to his room, got drunker, come out, and picked a fight. When he reached for a six-gun, Frank Flaherty, the night marshal, put a forty-five slug through Clyde's brisket. They buried him in Boot Hill 's morning. Corpses don't keep very good in this weather, y'know." The man laughed again. Lark guessed that the frequent laughter was a way of showing the opulence of the gold canines which decorated each side of the upper jaw.

"Guess I'll take the run back to the Gap, then, Mr. . . ."

"Parchman, Ben Parchman. But, Lark, seeing that I'm the manager here, I'll be the one to decide who handles valuable Robbins and Tucker property. So just who are you, and where do you come from?"

Lark stared at the man for a moment, then he said, "Forget it, pal. I'll rent me a nag at the livery to go back. Your stage can sit right out there until Christmas, for all of me."

The manager shrank visibly. "Now wait, wait a minute, Lark. No offense. I guess if you satisfied Miss Woodford, you satisfy me. After that holdup and all yesterday—well, just trying to do my job, that's all."

"I understand, Parchman. I'll stay with it, then. Just tell me where your stables are so I can change teams. I'll come back at departure time."

"It's on up the side street a furlong or so. You'll see our sign on the gate. Gimpy the hostler's there, prob'ly sleeping. Now, don't dawdle too long, Lark." Parchman had regained his official aplomb. "Stage leaves at two o'clock sharp. We don't dare miss our connection with the eastbound from Fort Ruskin, or there'd be the very Old Nick to pay."

"I think I can take care of all the chores in two hours," Lark said dryly, glancing at the boldfaced Seth Thomas ticking on the wall. Parchman looked at him sourly, but made no further comment. Lark went out.

He took his rig up the hill to the stables and turned it over to the hostler, a beat-up old wrangler with red-rimmed eyes, a stubble of whiskers, and a K-leg that had been broken and set badly long ago. The old man promised to have the fresh horses harnessed and ready at a quarter of two. Lark said, "Thanks, pardner, see you later," and went down the hill.

He looked up the main street from the corner by the stage station, and saw, a block above, a large building with an imposing sign creaking in the light breeze. It proclaimed:

THE RANK & FILE SALOON
ART RANKINE, PROP.

Lark walked up to it and turned in, the swinging doors whuff-whuffing closed behind him. He stood blinking for a moment, the long room dim after the brilliance of the noon sunshine. He saw that the place was clean enough, a bar extending all along one side, the floor covered with sawdust slightly redolent of resin, the odors of beer and whisky strong but not offensive. The tables along the wall opposite the bar were unoccupied, except for one near the door where a drunk dozed, his hat fallen off, his head crumpled on a bent forearm.

A long bartender stood at the center of the bar. Lark said, "Beer," and waited patiently while the paunchy man took his time drawing the foamy brew. The bartender took off the head of foam with a skimmer, then filled the mug from the tap again. He slid the mug down the bar to Lark, and Lark paid, leaving his change on the damp surface of the mahogany.

Two men—who had been playing a desultory game of pool at the single table in the very end of the room —stopped now. Without ostentation they racked their cues and came along the bar. The burly, dark-haired man hooked a boot over the brass rail at one side of Lark. The smaller, lighthaired man moved in on the other. Lark sipped his beer, turning to take a look at each of them in turn.

The big man was black Irish, Lark decided, a laboring man gone to seed. It'd been a long time since he'd held a gobstick in those hands. The other man was slim, taut, every motion controlled—make a good gunfighter, Lark thought, and maybe he is. With the most economical of motions, the slim man nudged the front

26

of his unbuttoned jacket so it fell open far enough to reveal a silver shield reading CITY MARSHAL.

Lark took a small measure of amusement from waiting them out. The minutes stretched and curled, while the fat bartender rested his heavy hams against the back bar, his face blank, polishing and repolishing the same glass interminably.

In the end, Lark won. The slender man cleared his throat and said, "Don't believe I've seen you in Magma before, mister."

Lark nodded. "That's not strange. Today's my first visit," he said amiably. "I brought the stage wagon in from the Gap this morning, and I guess I'll have to take the return run, too, from what Parchman tells me."

"That's right," the marshal said. "Prettiman got himself killed last night. By the way, I'm Art Rankine. I own this place, also serve as day marshal. This here is Frank Flaherty, my assistant, night marshal most of the time."

Lark nodded, not offering to shake hands. "I'm Justin Lark, gentlemen. I suppose I should thank you, Flaherty, for letting daylight into Clyde Prettiman. I needed the job."

The Irishman snorted. "Hell of a way to put it. You make it sound as if I enjoyed doin' it."

"Oh, nothing like that," Lark said. "Just a comment. I never knew Prettiman, so when his sudden demise gives me a steady job, I can't mourn him greatly."

"Oh, I see," Flaherty said, still scowling. "You're working for Rimi Woodford, then."

"I am if she'll keep me on. I blew into the Gap last night from Mantoul. I had a kind of half-assed job there, dealing in a joint, but the town voted in a reform bunch that closed the games down tighter than a Scotchman's wallet. So I decided to see what was on the other side of the mountain. Got as far as Coryell; somebody slugged me in an alley there. I woke up with a headache, and damn lucky that my ticket to the Gap and a double eagle were still hid out in my boot. Good thing I left the yellow boy there; we got held up in Dead Man's Canyon and they didn't find it. So that's my sad story, gents." Lark spread his palms flat on the bar, smiling at the two men.

"Heard about that holdup. Redtops, eh?" Rankine asked.

"So they say," Lark told him.

Rankine looked at him, rubbing a palm along his lean jaw. Then, as if satisfied, he motioned to the bartender. The man brought Lark another beer, a double whisky for Flaherty, and a bottle of lemon soda for Rankine.

"I never drink on duty," Rankine explained as he poured the soft drink. "You're a gambler, Lark?"

"Aren't we all, in this life?" Lark asked, sipping his beer. "But I've worked the profitable side of the table now and again. And I've done some mining, a bit of assaying, punched cattle when I had to. I've been a bank teller and a prison guard and a short-order cook. I can handle the ribbons on a four- or six- or eight-horse hitch. I've skinned mules and whacked bulls, though I hated that last. And one time I went eight rounds with Farmer Phillips before he knocked me kicking. You name it, Rankine, and I'll take a crack at it."

"Versatile, eh?" Rankine said, smiling at last. "Well, good for you. You'll need a lot of skills if you stick around this country. She's rough and tough and hard to curry."

"If my experience in Coryell and the Canyon is a good sample, I'll go along with you," Lark said. "You say it's even tougher this side of the Running Wolfs?"

"Coryell is an itty-bitty Sunday school, compared with Magma and Copperton, and Fort Ruskin ain't so damned far behind," Rankine said. "So keep your eyes peeled, mister, and whenever your rig is carrying anything in the strongbox worth more'n six bits, make sure that Ben Parchman hires a couple of gunslingers to ride shotgun with you."

"Rankine, I swear you're making me nervous," Lark said. "Until yesterday, I thought they'd tamed the West as far as holdups and such were concerned. Down in Denver the story was they caught all the highwaymen and hung 'em."

"Hung 'em? Lark, they've hung just three men in five years," Rankine said, with an edge of unexpected bitterness in his voice. "And there's been a score of honest citizens murdered. The only man who made any progress against the gangs was Sheriff Herold Martin. So a while back, they killed him, too. The man who took Martin's place, Pete Looby—why, Pete couldn't catch a fly with a barrel of molasses. And I swear he don't want to, either."

Lark shook his head. "I can't believe it. Why, thirty years ago they would have organized a vigilante band, and put an end to these Redtops quicker than scat."

"Vigilantes ain't much better than the bandits," Rankine said sourly. "They start paying off private debts. But the hell with it—me'n Frank here, and my jailer, we'll furnish all the law and order Magma needs. We'll leave the rest of Antelope County to look out for itself. Which it will have to do as long as Pete Looby is ramrodding the law."

"I guess your law in Magma is swift and sure, anyhow," Lark said. "I'm thinking of Clyde Prettiman."

Flaherty frowned, and emptied his glass. He said, "That was a hell of a thing. Clyde was drinking, and pretty shaky tryin' to get over it. A guy came to find me, said Clyde was over to the Bonanza, terrorizin' the place. Sure enough, there Clyde was, yellin' and cussin' and wavin' his six-gun. He takes one shot at a lamp, and misses. I yells, 'Clyde, put it down!' and he turns around and hollers, 'Frank, leave me alone or I'll have all the Bailors and Prettimans and Sumters come in here, and they'll plain wreck your Goddamn town!' I starts to say, 'Now, Clyde . . .' when he cuts loose a shot at me that just misses my ear. So naturally I had to kill him. Hated to. Clyde wasn't a bad sorta guy—sober, that is. All the Bailors and their clan go hog-wild when they get a skinful."

"Big bunch of 'em, all related?" Lark asked.

"Yeah," Rankine said, shaking his head. "Some pretty decent folks among 'em, but the Bailors especially—hardcases from away back. They do a little 'shining, rustle a few steers—never eat their own beef —steal horses here and there and peddle 'em, raise hell in general. Martin never managed to pin anything on 'em, solid, that is, and I haven't either. Gang took the bank here in Magma a few years ago; I still suspect they could have been in on that, and I ain't give up on it.

Anyhow, far as they are concerned, I got a line drawn around Magma they ain't s'posed to cross, and I got the yellow up the Bailors' necks high enough so they don't try it. Except for things like funerals, maybe."

"They sound like a bunch I'll steer clear of, then," Lark said. "I'm a scary sort of bird, gentlemen, and I value my skin too much to have people shoot holes in it. It's got to do me the rest of my life. Say, I enjoyed meeting you fellows, the talk and such. And thanks for the beer. Feller likes to have the lowdown on the higher-ups, like the man says, when he's in strange territory. Tell me, where's a good place to eat?"

"Why, the Little Bear's as good as any, maybe better," Rankine said. "Just up the street, second crosswalk."

"Odd name for a restaurant," Lark said.

Rankine laughed. "You remember, the little bear's porridge was so good that Goldilocks ate it all up? Town joke—the two mines at the top of the hill are the Big Bear and the Middle Bear. Was a Little Bear once, just below 'em, but after they taken a million in gold out of her, they hit borrasca and shut Little Bear down for good."

"Quite a story. Well, thanks again, men. I don't doubt but I'll be seeing you often, if I can handle this job," Lark said, and picked up his change from the bar.

4

Magma, M.T.
June 28, 1887

Dear Aunt Susan:
    All goes well. Have made some valuable acquaintances. My curiosity aroused about deaths of

Claude and John Woodford, and demise of Sheriff Herold Martin, Antelope County, all late 1885. Perhaps in your Wild West files you can find clips from Fort Ruskin Ledger or Copperton Miner with details of these sad events. The clips in your packet forwarded from Mantoul have little new. I think the Fourth Estate of this Territory writes its stories in the back room of a saloon with pencil and a pint of whisky! Not much for a man to get his teeth into in them.

Now have friends on stage lines; if I have a story I want to reach you fast, will have them relay by telegraph from one end of the stage line or the other. I approve your careful writing; the mails are uncertain, and I do not know the local lineup as yet. I can puzzle out the meaning.

Your aff. nephew,
Justin

<<<<<<<<<<<<<<<<<<<<<<<<<<<<<<<<<

The counter at the Little Bear restaurant was filled, but Lark found an empty table. He hung his hat on a hook and sat down with his back to the wall. Magma runs on the schedule of the mines, he thought; dinner twelve to one at home or boarding house. He looked about, finding it odd that among these diners he recognized not one familiar face. It was not odd, of course. He felt that he had gone through this before because he was in the warmup stage of the old familiar game. Later he would reduce the mystery to a mere puzzle. Then would come a loose end to grasp, then another . . .

Was there a lead in Parchman? The irascible little manager might be the most honest of men, or he might sit in his office day after day, resentful of his small salary, watching others get rich, scrabbling for some way to feather his own nest. He would have information which could be sold at a profit, if he knew the right—or rather the wrong—people. Lark made a check against Parchman in his mental book, as a man to be looked into farther. The tip that triggered the

Redtop holdup might not have come from Mantoul, after all.

"Can I help you, mister?" a woman's voice asked, and startled, Lark looked up at the girl standing beside him. A small girl, neatly built, her hair darkly red, her complexion fair, a few freckles sprinkled over the bridge of her nose. He looked again—he had seen this girl before. No, he amended, someone like her. Then he had it—Buzz Bailor, the intruder last night at the inn. Though the man had been of larger frame, she was built like him, compact and facile of movement. Her coloring was the same, the configuration of the facial planes. This girl had to be a Bailor.

"No menu? Then I'll have steak with onions, mashed potatoes, string beans, and apple pie," he said. "And coffee."

"That's just what we've got," she said, smiling. "Except the steak is venison."

"Then tell the cook to fry it well and pile on the onions. I've got good teeth."

"You'll need 'em," the girl said, and went through the swinging door into the kitchen.

Lark felt a little lift of excitement. What's a Bailor doing here in Magma, and how much does she know? Is this a loose end of the cat's-cradle that I'm trying to thread? He was still trying to devise an opening when she returned with his order and placed the dishes in front of him.

He saw that she had a certain awkwardness, not the facile manipulation of the experienced hash slinger. New here, he thought, as he tackled the food. She had been right; the steak was tough, the mashed potatoes lumpy. But though it lacked appeal, the food was fuel for Lark's furnace, and he went to work on it manfully.

When the girl brought the graniteware pot to fill his coffee cup, he asked casually, "Aren't you Miss Bailor?"

She almost dropped the big pot. "How did you know?"

"I met your brother recently. There's a family resemblance."

"Buzz it was, then—he's the only Bailor who really

32

looks like me. What of it, mister? If you are any friend to Buzz . . ." Her tone flattened into belligerence and an overtone of fear.

Lark gambled—here's this pretty girl, gone from the family ranch, working in Magma. He said, "We're far from friends. We had an argument, and I had to take his gun and his knife away from him. I've got the feeling your brother doesn't like me whatever."

"You're lucky," she said, and added, contempt in her voice, "My brother Buzz, mister, is a rat and a no-good. He's plain scum. Buzz is the big reason I left home for good."

"Too bad you had to make a break like that," Lark said, his voice kindly. "Family's important—help one another, work together, you know, lift each other over the rough spots, affection . . ."

"You don't know our shiftless bunch that men call the Bailors," the girl said fiercely. "They were bad enough when mamma was alive, but she died five years ago. I managed to put up with the dirt and the meanness and the filthy ways until a couple of months ago. But when Buzz got me into the barn and tried to —tried to—his own sister, mind you—I couldn't stand it no longer. I run away and come here."

"They haven't bothered you in Magma?" Lark asked.

"Not yet. They stay pretty much away from Magma; they're scairt of Art Rankine. He hates their guts and they hate his. But there's a few of 'em in town today. They come for Clyde's funeral; somebody got word to 'em about it. They got Clyde buried this morning, but the clan ain't pulled out yet; they're taking advantage of the marshal letting 'em come in for the funeral. And I'll betcha they're hurrying to get drunk right now. Drunk with a Bailor or a Prettiman or a Sumter, that means trouble, nothin' but trouble." She stared out the front window toward the street, her pretty face clouded, biting her lower lip. At last she came back to the present and said, "Sorry, mister, my problems. I'll get your pie."

He finished the pie, which was mediocre, and leaving a generous tip, reached for his hat. He was paying his check at the front counter when the door slammed open wide. Two men came in, one big, redhaired,

33

rawboned, mean of eye and mouth. The other man was younger, a smaller copy, but not as hard-looking.

"Where's Lolly?" the big man roared. "Lolly, you little bitch, come out here!"

The older woman who had taken Lark's money stared at the man, her face stark with fear. "What— what do you want Lolly for?" she stammered.

Lark, standing unobtrusively beside the counter, heard a scraping of chairs as the few remaining noon patrons abandoned their food. Though Lark did not turn, he caught the hurried tread of bootsoles as the men hastened out the rear door. Good, he thought— clear the joint, and if I have to take this redhead, no-body else will get hurt.

"Why, because she's goin' home to the ranch, by God!" the big man shouted. "Where is . . . oh, there you are, my stuck-up sister! Come along, you're gettin' out of this swill-hole right now."

Turning his head, Lark saw that Lolly Bailor had come from the kitchen. She stood still, wiping her hands on her apron. There was a set, angry look on her face, but no sign of fear. She came forward and planted herself solidly in front of the man. She pointed a finger at him.

"Anse Bailor, will you shut your fat noisy mouth and get out of here? You too, Marsh. This minute. The very idea, coming into the place where I work and making such a God-awful fuss! You should be ashamed of yourselves."

Anse Bailor's belligerence faded a little. "We're tired of eatin' the slop that squaw of pa's dishes up for us," he growled. "We're takin' you back, Lolly. You don't belong in this town. First thing we know, we're gonna hear that you've started hookin' on the Line."

Lolly's hand swung like the lash of a whip and caught Anse across the side of the face. "So that's what you think of your sister!" she cried. "Now I know I'll never, never go back to Box B!"

"The hell you won't! When Pike Sumter come out last night to tell us Clyde got kilt, he told us about seein' you here, and what you been doin' and all. So paw says to get you t'hell home. Come along, missy!"

34

His big hand reached out and caught her slender wrist, twisting cruelly. The girl cried out in pain.

Far enough, Lark thought. In that first automatic appraisal of the two men, he had seen that Anse wore a six-gun, but Marsh was unarmed. His hand went unobtrusively to the buttons of his jacket and opened it. Then he stepped forward.

Anse Bailor was trying to drag his sister to the door, but she was resisting with surprising strength for such a small girl. Lark brought the edge of his hand down hard on the wrist of Bailor. The big man yelled and his hand dropped away from the girl. He stood massaging the wrist with his other hand, glaring at Lark.

"Sister or not, you leave this girl alone," Lark said in icy tones. "If she doesn't want to go, you're not going to force her. You want to go with them, miss?"

She looked at him, her eyes misty with tears. She turned her head toward Anse, then the younger man. She drew herself up to her full height. "I do not want to go," she said firmly.

"You heard her, boys," Lark said. "Now get out of here and leave her alone. I won't tell you again."

No weapon, no threat, but the lash of authority in Lark's voice beat down the bluster of Anse Bailor. Marsh Bailor clinched it when he urged, "C'mon, Anse. Let's get out of here. We can . . ."

What they could do was drowned out in the tinkle of the little bell on the door as Marsh swung it open. The two clumped out, leaving the door swinging wide. Lark closed it gently.

"Thanks, mister, but they'll be back," the girl said, with an edge of desperation in her voice. "They'll keep thinking about it, and they'll find a saloon and get some more Dutch courage under their belts, and they'll come back. They'll drag me away by force. And if you interfere, they'll kill you."

"You're sure they'll be at you again?" Lark said.

"I know them; they're my brothers," Lolly said bitterly.

Behind them they heard an ostentatious clearing of throat. Turning, Lark saw the woman who evidently was the proprietor holding out a slender fold of green-

35

backs. "Here's your pay, girl. I can't have rowdies like that busting up my business. So the quicker you get out of here the better I'll like it."

"Please, Mrs. Drucker, wasn't my work all right?" the girl asked.

"Yes, yes, but—oh, I made a mistake when I took you on. Everybody knows the Bailors, and . . . well . . ."

"I understand," Lolly said. She took off her apron, her head high in disdain. But she stood for a moment as if uncertain of her next move.

Lark said, "Miss Bailor, go up to your room, wherever it is, and pack your belongings. Bring them down to the stage station. The stage to Stoneman's Gap leaves in twenty minutes, and I'll be driving it. You've got to get out of this town."

She stared at him, irresolute. But something in his manner inspired her confidence, and she had no alternative. She nodded and stuffed the little wad of bills down the front of her dress. "Goodbye, Mrs. Drucker," she said. Taking her cape from a hook in the back hall, she hurried toward the back door. The door closed softly behind her.

Lark said to the woman, "Mrs. Drucker, I can't say that I blame you, but I will say I don't particularly admire you. Now there is one thing you owe that girl —if anyone asks you where she went, you can say you don't know, she just ran out the back door and was gone. You will say that, won't you?" He had not raised his voice, but the steely edge of his tone touched the woman. She recoiled, staring at him, then she nodded slowly. Lark smiled at her and went out the front door.

He headed toward the stage station. Halfway down the block he stopped, boot soles planted firmly on the wooden sidewalk. Coming toward him were Anse and Marsh Bailor, the big man hunched forward, like a great clumsy bear. Marsh tagged behind, as if reluctant to join in whatever might be his brother's purpose. They hadn't taken as long as Lolly guessed for stoking up, Lark thought; I suppose they had well celebrated the interment of Clyde Prettiman.

"So there you are, wise guy," Anse said, stopping on

36

the plank walk in front of Lark. He swayed a little. "Where's Lolly?"

Lark shrugged. "Why don't you let the girl alone?"

"Because she's m'sister, by God, and she ain't gonna make a fool out of me in front of the whole town of Magma!"

"She couldn't make a fool out of you, Anse," Lark said pleasantly. "God in his infinite mercy did that when he let you be born."

His fingers flicked hard to the brim of Anse's hat. As the man's hand went instinctively to the dislodged hat, Lark's knee dropped behind the man's leg. A sweep of the arm, and Anse went stumbling back over the edge of the high wooden sidewalk. He landed sitting, with a bone-jolting jar, in the gravel of the street. He sat there, his mouth open, gasping like a fish out of water.

Lark reached out and clamped an iron grip on the shoulder of the younger man. "Don't do it, Marsh," he warned softly.

"I ain't—ain't doin' nothin', mister," Marsh said hurriedly. "This is Anse's game. I ain't takin' no cards in it. Lolly's a good kid. Anse and Buzz have always bullied her, but not me. If you can help her, well and good." He drew aside, shrinking back into the thin ring of spectators already gathered. He said, "Look out, mister. Anse has got a gun."

The watchers scattered like hens at the shadow of a hawk. Anse, staggering erect, fumbled for his six-gun. He looked up at Lark, standing above him on the walk. "You ast for it, nosy, so now I'm gonna kill you."

The derringer in Lark's armpit was an ace in the hole, and he didn't think it was needed yet. Instead, he moved to the edge of the sidewalk, his boots firm on the splintery boards. The exact sequence of his moves flashed through his mind.

But he did not move yet, for he heard the solid clump of boots along the boards. He did not turn his head, but he saw Anse Bailor's head swivel toward the sound, the pistol barrel wavering. A voice demanded, "What's going on here?" Art Rankine's voice, Lark recognized—the voice of authority.

"Gonna kill this son-of-a-bitch," Anse said harshly.

"Gun him down, eh? And him unarmed?" the marshal asked, his voice level. "Y'know, Bailor, the law counts that murder here in Antelope County. You want to hang by the neck?" He leaned down and put a hand on the edge of the walkway and vaulted to the street level below.

"Law, you say? Law don't signify when a man comes between a feller and his own sister. This nosy bastard has shoved his beak into Bailor family affairs, and I'm gonna see that he's not around to do it again, never."

"Murder, Anse, murder—remember?" the marshal said, taking two steps toward the man.

Anse snorted. "Law cain't touch me, marshal; I'm a Bailor. The law's a joke—you want to see me prove it?" To Lark he said, "All right, nosy, stand up like a man and take it, for I'm aimin' to kill you."

The marshal moved with smooth precision. The leather slungshot in his hand took Anse Bailor just over the right ear. Without a sound, the big man went down like a poleaxed ox into the dust. The crowd surged forward, staring down at the fallen man, eyes bulging like frogs in a swamp. The marshal looked up at them, with a thin smile.

"Fergy, that your rig there?" he asked. One of the onlookers nodded. Stooping to pick up Bailor's pistol, the marshal said, "All right, get this hardcase loaded into it and haul him down to the hoosegow. I'll be down there in a few minutes."

"But—but . . ." the man sputtered.

"Nothing to worry about," the marshal said calmly. "He won't be coming to for a while, and then he'll have such a splitting headache he won't be in the mood to bother anybody. So get going."

As several men jumped down to help Fergy load the inert Anse into the back of Fergy's buggy, the marshal vaulted up to the walk and joined Lark. He stood watching the men, slapping the leather slungshot lightly into the open palm of his other hand. "Full of BB shot," he observed. "Plenty of weight but it don't bust the skin. Handy little life preserver."

38

"It is that," Lark said. "Thanks, Rankine. No telling what a half-drunk will do."

"Not when he's a Bailor, anyhow. But I don't think you were much worried, mister," the marshal said, again with that thin smile. "I had half a notion to let you handle him; I've got the feeling it would have been a pleasure to watch you. But there's always the element of luck. Your foot might have slipped, the kid brother might have decided to take a hand. It wasn't worth a good man getting hurt. So I stepped in to settle it."

"With efficiency and dispatch," Lark said, grinning. He thrust a hand out to Rankine. "Maybe I can reciprocate some day. By the way, I'm taking the sister down to the Gap. I'm sure Miss Rimi can use the help, and the girl isn't safe in Magma. All on the QT, of course."

"That's the pretty little girl, Lolly, that's been working at the Little Bear? She's what all the trouble was about? You got the right idea, Lark, taking her away. Magma's a tough town for a lone girl, and one with family troubles besides. The Bailors won't bother her down at the Gap."

Lark must have shown his surprise. "Some special charm?"

The marshal laughed. "When old Willis Stoneman owned that property at the Gap before he sold to Claude Woodford, the Bailors decided they wanted the place. They tried to run the old man off his homestead. Willis grabbed a loaded Spencer and killed Cock Bailor. Then he blew the middle finger off Lippy's hand, and busted Anse's leg. They never tried anything there again; they fight shy of the place like it was the plague. Except maybe Buzz and Marsh, who were too young to have participated in that sad lesson. No, Lolly should be safe enough at the Inn."

"Good, real good," Lark said. He glanced at his watch. "Well, I'd better get going, or Ben Parchman will have a conniption." He started to turn away, then asked in a low voice, "Marshal, what did Anse mean when he said the law can't touch a Bailor?"

"He's not far wrong," Rankine said, his voice flat. "It's a long story, and one I don't much like. I'll give you all the dirty details one of these days, if you're interested."

Lark looked squarely at the marshal. Then he nodded, deciding there was little more to be gained at this time. "I'm interested," he said. "See you soon, marshal." He turned, and without a backward look went up the hill toward the Robbins and Tucker stables.

When he brought the stage wagon to a stop at the brick building, he found Lolly Bailor waiting inside the depot, sitting demurely on one of the hard benches. There were three other passengers—a whisky drummer for Mantoul, a hardrock miner with an injured hand bound for Butte City, and a woman from Fort Ruskin who had been visiting her married daughter.

"You all set, Miss Bailor?" Lark asked the girl.

She nodded, flicking a glance at the battered wicker suitcase secured with a piece of rope. "All my worldly goods," she said with a shaky smile. Lark smiled back. Kid's got a sense of humor, he thought.

"Anse is safe in jail for a while," he said in a low voice. "Marsh has gone on home, I think. He told me he had tried to stop Anse. The boy seems to be fond of you."

"The only one of my family who ever helped me or gave me a kind word," she said.

The next few minutes were filled with the bustle of loading the baggage into the boot, getting the passengers settled, and checking out the small amount of express. When the stage was ready, Lark and Parchman went back into the office.

"Parchman, does our company boast an armory?" Lark asked.

"Why, we have some guns, yes," Parchman said sourly. "But you haven't got anything valuable this trip. Why . . . ?"

"My life," Lark said. "Let me have that lever-action rifle there by the safe. It's loaded? Good. Don't worry, I'll sign for it." He scribbled his signature on the piece of paper Parchman gave him, and shoved it back across the counter. He took the gun, checked the magazine, and nodded. Glancing at the clock, he saw

40

it was two minutes until departure. He turned toward the door.

"Uh, Lark, the young lady, the one with the cloak . . ."

"What about her?"

"She hasn't bought a ticket. She didn't pay . . ."

Lark looked sharply at the manager. I could say I'm deadheading her, he thought, but if I do I'll make a mortal enemy of old fussbudget. And I might need him later. He's a cranky old counterjumper, but in his position as manager he might be learning things that I need to know.

He said, "The girl's holding pretty light, Parchman. Suppose I advance her fare and get it from her later? That OK?"

There was a shadow of a leer on the manager's face as he nodded. Lark paid him and took the change. Parchman slid down the rolltop of his desk and locked it. He twirled the dial of the safe to scatter the combination. He slammed shut the big ledger and put it into a cupboard. He was just peeling down the sateen sleeve protectors when Lark said, "Oh, Parchman, I'd better have a receipt for that fare, in case the girl forgets."

The manager glared at him, but Lark held his ground. Annoyed, Parchman unlocked and opened the desk, fumbled for a receipt book, sat down and made it out. He tore out the slip and handed it to Lark as if it were a venomous snake. Lark took it, and smiling, walked out, the rifle cradled under his arm.

Exactly on the stroke of two, the Robbins and Tucker stage wagon rumbled down the main street of Magma, its four passengers inside, and Justin Lark on the high box, the reins threaded through the fingers of his left hand, his right hand cracking his whiplash like pistol shots over the four horses. And on the floor of the box, just under his boots, rested the loaded .30-30 rifle.

5

Dear Aunt Susan:

A quiet Sunday, no stage run. I am now regular driver, an orchestra seat for any passing show. To-morrow, though, young Phil Woodford will take the shuttle to Magma, as I volunteered to stay at the Inn with Miss Rimi. Also staying is Miss Lolita Bailor who is now employed here and is somewhat indebted to me. Everyone else from here, and the whole country in fact, will go to Magma to celebrate the Glorious Fourth, with horse races, fireworks, beer, and skittles, and I'm sure many fine long speeches extolling the reasons Montana should be admitted to the Union as a state.

A few pieces of my project now fitting together. I find I need badly the historical information I asked for. Send also the suitcase with my spare clothes; I need them as well. I am looking forward to having those old friends of yours drop in on me soon. I have made a few new enemies.

Your aff. nephew,
Justin

<<<<<<<<<<<<<<<<<<<<<<<<<<<<<<<<<<<

At Rimi Woodford's insistence, Lark had moved from his cubicle in the bunkhouse into a room in the help's quarters of the inn. He was pleased at her request, for he was beginning to accumulate papers and other material he did not like to have subjected to prying eyes. Moreover, Rimi had said, "I'll tell you

42

the truth of it, Justin, I feel more secure with a grown man in the house. I didn't care to have Clyde Prettiman around, but you—well, you're different. After the way you handled Buzz Bailor—and they tell me Anse Bailor as well—I'm able to get more rest at night than I ever have since dad and Uncle John were—were killed."

"I'd like to hear about that sometime," he had told her. "All right, I'll move up here. It will be handier all around."

Now he sealed the letter to his aunt and walked from his room down the hall and across the lobby. Rimi Woodford was working in the post-office corner. She looked up, smiling, and he thought, almost with surprise, "What a pretty girl she is."

He held out coins. "Could I make a large purchase, Miss Rimi? Ten two-cent stamps, please."

She counted out the stamps and handed them to him. He detached one, licked it, and stuck it on the corner of his envelope. He handed her the letter and she read the superscription aloud: "Miss Susan Eames, Box Three Four Three, Denver, Colorado." As she dropped it into one of the four open mail sacks hanging below the letter rack, she asked, "Your lady friend, Justin?"

"In a way, yes," he said with a chuckle. "My old maid aunt, who still looks on me as six years old, a boy who must be supervised for his own good. She's crippled and doesn't get out much, so she dotes on what I am doing, where I go, the people I meet. I try to write her every day. She's a dear thing."

"You're not married, then?" The question was casual.

"No, nor ever have been. I guess I move around too much to have any time for courting. Though I suppose some day I'll settle down. But you, Rimi—I'd think a pretty girl like you would have a string of suitors a mile long beating a path to Stoneman's Inn."

She laughed. "I'm neither that pretty nor that popular, Justin. I guess I'm married to this place . . ." She swept an arm toward the parlor and the lobby. "Day in, day out, from dawn to dusk. I don't have much time left for romance. Mind you, I'm not complaining—the inn is a good living for me and the two children who depend on me. I find it interesting and challenging. But I would like to get away now and then. And there are—well, certain other things, frightening things . . ." She stopped, with a little shake of the head.

Now? he thought. He looked around at the quiet empty rooms. "Are you busy right now, Rimi? I'd like to talk."

"I'm not rushed. The Fort Ruskin stage will be here for a lunch stop at noon. We'll feed the passengers, switch teams, I'll put on the Mantoul mail sack and take off the local mail. Then, thank goodness, we're through for this day. No evening stages tonight because of the Fourth tomorrow, so I can take it easy except for a dozen things I have been postponing."

"How's Lolly doing? Is she pulling her weight?"

"Justin, the girl's a jewel. I wasn't enthusiastic at first; I guess I was prejudiced against anyone named Bailor. But she's—well, she's different. She wants to better herself. She has already asked me if she can borrow some of Phil's school books. She never had a chance to go beyond the third reader in her whole life. I gather that after her mother died, living at Box B was like living with a bunch of animals. She does speak well of her brother Marsh, but for the rest, even her father, she has contempt and hate. Justin, I find that hard to understand. My own father was stern but just. And he had a fine sense of humor. Though we had our off moments, we all loved each other, and our little quarrels were quickly patched up. So to hate your father and your brothers as bitterly as Lolly hates hers, I find a sad, sad thing, Justin."

"I'm glad the girl is out of that atmosphere," he said. "Rimi, tell me about your father and your uncle."

She glanced up at the wall clock, whose dial was the inexorable master of life at the inn. She said, "It's a long story, and it still hurts me, but I'll take the time. My father, Justin, was a mechanic from the East who came up the river by steamboat in the sixties, seeking his fortune in the gold fields. He met my mother in Helena and married her. As he moved around the camps, she went along—a hard life, but they loved each other. I was born at Rimini, near Helena, and it tickled my father to name me after that camp. Phil was born at Philipsburg, and Goldie at Gold Creek. My father never suffered from lack of work, for he could do anything with his hands. And he saved his money, for he had a dream." She paused, drawing a deep breath. "Always, Justin, in the back of his mind, he wanted to own an inn, a handsome busy posthouse such as he had known as a boy. Those inn-keepers were big men in the community, looked up to, admired."

"We all have dreams," Lark said. "I yearned to become a railroad engineer, but I never made it."

"His dream looked pretty remote for dad, too, in spite of the money he saved," she said. "Then, after Goldie was born, my mother went into a decline. She caught pneumonia and died at a forgotten mining camp in the mountains. When dad was digging a grave for her on the hillside, he struck a sizeable pocket of gold. The cleanup gave enough to start the financing of this inn, though he was several years in finding the exact location he wanted. Even when he found this place, old Willis Stoneman, who owned the land and the log tavern here, didn't want to sell. Then the Bailors tried to run Stoneman off to get the Gap for themselves. Stoneman killed one of them and injured two more. That must have convinced him, for he took father's offer and moved away to Fort Ruskin."

"I heard about that dustup," Lark said.

"When the papers were signed, dad sent for his brother John to come out from Wisconsin. The two of them built the inn. They were both perfectionists, so our inn is one of the finest buildings in all of the Territory. But then they struck trouble—neither of them were businessmen. They were too generous with credit; they couldn't drive a hard bargain. Justin, I've learned to do those things, learned because it was root hog or die after my men were killed. It's been hard, terribly hard, but I'm getting the place back on its feet. I've paid off one loan, and I can see daylight on the rest. Our bankers in Fort Ruskin got me the post office, and that has been a godsend."

45

"You've hoed a hard row, and that's for certain sure. How long have you been the head ramrod?"

"Just about a year and a half. Dad and Uncle John were murdered in November of eighty-five. Justin, they said it was Indians, because the two men were stripped naked and scalped. But I've never been convinced. Dad and Uncle John had been to Fort Ruskin and were on their way back when it happened. There hadn't been even one report of renegade Indian braves seen off the reservation for months, then or later. To cap the horror of it, only a few days later, Sheriff Martin's drowned body was found in Cornish Creek, north of the Rail Fence ranch. And that is a hundred miles south of his office at Fort Ruskin."

"That's strange," Lark said, frowning. "Did anyone ever find a connection?"

She shook her head. "But from something my father said, I'm sure his main reason for going to Fort Ruskin was to consult the sheriff. If he did, and Sheriff Martin was following up on whatever information dad had given him, it must have been some terrible thing, for the three of them to be killed because of it. Oh, Justin, it's all so terrifying! This beautiful country should be prosperous and pleasant and friendly. Instead, it's like a festering sore, all rotten underneath the surface. The man who comes down the road may be an honest cowboy, or he may be one of the Redtops, ready to rob and kill. Nobody feels safe in property, or person, or even life." She stopped, looking at him with a sad smile, but with seeming relief, as if she had held this outburst back for a long time, and was glad to unburden herself of it now.

Lark put his callused hand over her small one as it lay on the counter. "Rimi, I've only been here a few days, but I've felt it too—something ugly, suspicion and fear and things hidden. I've seen men who should be behind bars walking about openly. I feel that I should do something to put an end to it."

She looked at him squarely, her eyes sincere and unwavering. "Justin, against my own best interests, against my own deep feelings, I must advise you— please pack your things, get on the next stage for Mantoul, and go away for good. This country isn't safe

46

for anyone with heart and conscience as you have. I mean it, Justin. I'll even—even give you the money for your ticket."

He patted her hand and let it go. "Rimi, I couldn't pull out in the face of trouble, your trouble. Oh no, my pretty maid. It may be dangerous, but it's a puzzle that intrigues me. I'd have to have much greater reason before I'd run like a rabbit. You're staying; why shouldn't I?"

"Because it's a new game to you, while I know the cards and some of the players. And I can't abandon my inn—it's a millstone around my neck, but I love it, and it's Phil and Goldie's heritage, too. But there are times . . . Justin, I'll tell you in the utmost secrecy, I would be able to leave—I have a bonafide buyer for the inn and all the Gap property. For cash."

He looked at her in surprise. Is this the break I've been looking for? he wondered. The strategic location of the Gap, which had struck him the first moment he stepped off the stage, had not gone unnoticed by others. "Who's your buyer?" he asked.

She did not answer directly. "We have neighbors, Justin. I don't include the Bailors. But Ted Powell, who runs the XL, and his wife are good friends of ours. Tom Fredericks has a spread, the Anchor, some miles beyond. It's no great shakes, and Tom is getting old and crotchety; he may sell out. Then north, on the Fort Ruskin road, where Cornish Creek joins the Redstone, is Rail Fence. It's owned by Sascha Verloff, who came to the Territory from Europe. In a few years he's built Rail Fence into a prosperous ranch, taking over two other ranches adjoining his original property. People say Sascha was a count or some such in the old country. He has plenty of money—you should see the new ranchhouse at Rail Fence. It's a regular mansion, full of oil paintings and china and statues and such."

"He sounds interesting. I'd like to meet him," Lark said.

"You will," she said. "He and his sister Sonya are coming over this evening for dinner. I said I'd tell him then if I had decided to sell."

"So Verloff is your potential purchaser?"

47

"He is. Oh, it's a terrible temptation, Justin. The burdens of running this place are sometimes agonizing. But still, I love it, and I'd be lying if I said I didn't enjoy operating it, even with all its problems. It's the atmosphere, the outside happenings that frighten me."

"How would you feel if the Redtops were destroyed, the lawless element broken up and brought to book? The holdups and murders ended once and for all?"

"Why, I wouldn't consider selling for a single minute," she said without hesitation. "It would be like a different world. To live secure, in peace . . ." She looked at him sharply. "Why do these crimes have so much interest for you, Justin?"

He smiled at her and shook his head. "My dear girl, in my short stay I've learned that on this side of the Running Wolfs there are three major topics of conversation—the weather, the price of beef, and the latest atrocity of the Redtops gang. I'd have to be deaf not to have heard of this lawless threat."

"I suppose that's right," she said doubtfully, as if not quite satisfied. "I'm frightened, Justin, I think my best move would be to tell Sascha Verloff tonight that I'll sell him the inn."

Lark studied her face, knowing by her serious look that she did not relish the prospect. Neither did he —this unexpected development would destroy, at least for a time, the base he had been building up so carefully. He might have to start over with Verloff, and the man was an unknown quantity.

Knowing he was dissembling, knowing his advice was given to fit his own selfish ends, instead of the needs of Rimi Woodford, Lark said, "Rimi, why don't you put off the decision? With Lolly Bailor here, you may find your work load lighter. I'd hate to see you make a hasty move that you would regret later. There could be new developments, with the stage lines, the ranchers . . ."

"Unless you've heard something I haven't, unless you know more than you are telling, Justin, there's no help from those directions," she said, giving him a sharp look. Then she relented, laughing a little. "Oh, I'm being picky. But to ease your mind and mine, I

48

will postpone my decision for now. I'll tell Sascha—he won't like it, but he'll be too much the diplomat to show it."

"Good," Lark said, secretly relieved. "This Verloff sounds interesting. I'm looking forward to meeting him."

"You will, tonight. You knew about our little Fourth of July party? Well, not so little—half the county is coming: KL, Anchor, Rail Fence, the owners and their families and their cowhands. A real shindig. Justin, would you play your guitar for a while? We might be able to scare up a fiddle someplace."

"Sure, I'll lead some jigs and reels and come-all-ye's. Why, we'll make the very welkin ring, in honor of our nation's natal day a hundred and eleven years ago. But will we have a large enough contingent of the fair sex?"

"You'll be surprised. Ted Powell has three pretty daughters, Tom Fredericks will bring his housekeeper and her daughter. And the young punchers will find girls to bring, if they have to drive a buggy fifty miles to squire them here. And there's Sonya Verloff, Sascha's sister. You're in for a treat, Justin, meeting the Princess."

"A real princess?" Lark asked.

"I'm not sure—probably not, though everyone calls her that. She's a beautiful thing, but cold as ice. The clothes she wears—well, she makes me feel like a peasant."

"You can hold your own in any company, Rimi," Lark said gallantly. "But I do enjoy meeting beautiful women. When I give that up, it will be time to bury me. And I'm ready—Minnie Heavy Bear washed and ironed my other shirt. I'll be a real dude."

Rimi laughed, genuine amusement in the sound of it. Lark guessed that the postponement of a decision about selling the inn had given her relief from a chafing worry.

"I'm not sure Sonya is your type, Justin," she said. "Or you hers. But you have something in common, she's a talented musician."

"That lets me out, barnyard guitarist that I am," he said. "When does the party start?"

"The crowd will start arriving about eight. At midnight we'll have a potluck supper, and the dawn will be streaking the sky when the last guest leaves. Some of the people won't even go to bed; they'll drive right on to Magma for the big celebration."

"Sounds like fun. You look for any trouble from the Bailors—trying to crash the party, I mean?"

"God forbid. But I don't think they'd try it; too many tough and honest people around for them to handle. Most likely we'll have a few fistfights of our own, down behind the bunkhouse, but nothing serious. A black eye or two, a few loosened teeth, and the boys will make up again when they get sober. It's all a part of the Glorious Fourth."

"I've seen it before," Lark said, grinning. "I hope, though, that you make the guests check their guns."

"I do. I'd hate to see any whisky killings—or nearly as bad, to have some glass shot out of the inn. New window glass is too expensive, when it has to come by boat from St. Louis or by rail and bull-train from Bismarck."

"Since I'm not going to Magma, I'll help with the big cleanup in the morning," Lark said. "I guess on that account I ought to stick to lemon soda, like Art Rankine."

Smiling, she said, "You might. You've met Art? A good lawman; he keeps Magma right under his thumb, wild though it is. A few years ago the Redtops raided the Magma bank—there was a bank there then—and they shot down Charley Cloud, the banker, and nearly killed Art. Since then, Art has hated the lawless element with a dedicated passion. And they know it. They stay out of the town, and confine their dirty work to Dead Man's Canyon and the long miles of road to Copperton and Fort Ruskin and Coryell."

Lark would have liked to pursue the subject, but at that moment Lolly Bailor called, "Rimi, Minnie needs you in the kitchen." "Excuse me," Rimi said. Automatically, she locked the post-office till and dropped the key into her pocket. Nodding approval of her caution, Lark watched her hurry toward the kitchen with her straight proud walk.

Instead of following her employer, Lolly Bailor

stood uncertainly at the door of the dining room for a moment, then she crossed the lobby toward Lark. She looked up at him, her glance dropped shyly away, and her cheeks grew pink.

"Mr. Lark," she said in a low voice, "I just—just wanted to thank you for what you did for me. Miss Rimi is a dandy; she couldn't be nicer. And everything here is so clean and smells so nice, and there's books, and I ain't scairt all the time—why, Mr. Lark, to me it's like heaven! And I won't ever forget that you were the one who gave me the chance at it."

She's in the right mood, Lark thought—take advantage of it. "Don't mention it, Lolly," he said. "One of the pleasures of my life is helping pretty girls." He was rewarded by a deepening blush, and another shy smile. He went on, "There is something you can do for me. You see, I'm writing some stories I hope to sell someday to the eastern papers. Since you were born and raised in this country, you could tell me all about ranch life—the real thing, I mean. The day-to-day activities with the cattle, the storms, what you do in winter, things like that."

"Why, I'll be tickled to do what I can, Mr. Lark, but there ain't much about my ranch life that anybody would want to read about, I tell you. Cold and hot, dirty and wet, awful dull."

"Never any excitement at all, Lolly?" he asked, his tone light and teasing.

She gave him a direct look, her eyes narrowed. She said, very seriously, "Excitement there was at times, but it was all of a rotten picture with the rest—drinking, and gambling and . . . women, if you want to call them that. Those things, well, I don't think I could talk about them, Mr. Lark. But when we have a chance to work on it, you ask me questions and I'll try to answer."

"Nothing could be fairer, Lolly. We'll get together. Are you looking forward to the party tonight?"

She blushed again. "Mr. Lark, I'm nineteen years old. I scratched and scrabbled to get through the third reader, and learn to write and cipher. But I never learned no manners, or how to talk to folks, or how to eat nice in company. Mr. Lark, I never been to a

51

party in all my life. I'm scairt. Maybe I'll stay in my room with the door shut, so I won't make a fool of myself in front of all them folks."

Lark put an arm around her shoulders and gave her a light squeeze before releasing her. "Lolly, you'd disappoint all those handsome cowhands who are coming for miles to the party. No, no, honey. We'll see that you meet the right boys, and five minutes later you'll have forgotten all about being a shrinking violet. Believe me, Lolly, you'll find it all comes naturally."

"Gosh, I hope you're right, Mr. Lark," she said. "Would you—well, kinda look out for me?"

"You can count on me," Lark said, and watched smiling as the auburn-haired girl hurried back to the kitchen.

6

Stoneman's Gap, M.T.
July 4, 1887

Dear Aunt Susan:
Your telegram forwarded to me by stage yesterday, just before arrival of your friend Mr. Tetrault. We have gotten together and I will show him the high points of this region. He will stay here at the inn for a while.

Met two very interesting people, Sascha and Sonya Verloff, owners Rail Fence Ranch, handsome people of Polish descent, in early thirties. Lived at one time in Chicago; perhaps Uncle Allan might know them.

For our book—in Magma, Ben Parchman, manager for R & T Stage, should know much about refining and shipping of gold from Bear Consolidated. Not very communicative, however. My new friend, Art Rankine, city marshal of Magma, has many tall stories about lawbreakers. Will copy some of them down for you. Art is a fine lawman, and honest.

Party at the inn last night for all the countryside. Much good talk, played the guitar, dancing all night. Have slight headache this morning. Picked up info. that business we were interested in used to be divided among several firms, but now is under one head. Type of management not yet known, but working on it.

Have your friend Mr. Collins bring me that picture of you when he comes. It will be an inspiration to me.

I feel I am making progress, though slowly.

Your aff. nephew,

Justin

‹‹‹‹‹‹‹‹‹‹‹‹‹‹‹‹‹‹‹‹‹‹‹‹‹‹‹‹‹‹‹

The eastbound stage had rolled in from Fort Ruskin, its passengers had wolfed their lunches, and piled back into the Concord. To the cracking of the driver's whip, the big coach had lurched onto the main road and was gone into the gloomy depths of Dead Man's Canyon. Rimi Woodford had unlocked the mail sack and sorted the slim sheaf of mail, stuffing letters into the pigeonholes designated for the local ranches. She hung the Magma pouch on its hook and dropped in the letters being forwarded.

"Letter for you, Justin," she called across the lobby. "It looks like a telegraph envelope."

He tore the letter open and scanned the contents. "Right enough. It's a telegram forwarded from Fort Ruskin. My aunt Susan thinks an acquaintance of hers will be passing through here, and wires me to be on the lookout for him. Honestly, that woman—from her wheelchair she has tendrils reaching across half the world. There isn't anything she isn't interested in. What she likes most, what she dotes on, are tales of criminals and crimes, and the bloodier the crime, the better. She can call half the bandits and gunmen in the West by their first names—vicariously, of course."

"Too bad she can't live around Stoneman's Gap for

a while. She'd get violence in plenty," Rimi said, with a certain grimness.

"Auntie would glory in it. Say, Rimi, I'm going down to take care of the stock, to give Phil a break, since he's doing my driving tomorrow. Is your party all set?"

"All ready. Justin, I invited Sascha and his sister to come early and have dinner with us. And I want you, too."

"If you say so, though I'm not sure I know how to act in such high sassiety."

She smiled. "Of course you do. And I want your moral support, since I'm going to follow your suggestion and tell Sascha I haven't made up my mind yet. And you'll enjoy meeting the Princess."

"D'you think I should kiss her hand when I meet her?"

"She wouldn't turn a hair if you did. I'm afraid I haven't been quite fair in my description of Sonya. She *is* beautiful, and striking, and intelligent. I guess I'm a little jealous."

"She sounds quite awesome."

"Justin, she isn't at all. And you're not fooling me about being nervous; you're a man who's been around more than somewhat, in your better days. Even though you play the dumb cowpuncher or ignorant teamster."

"There's no universal yardstick to judge a man, pretty lady. It happens I was snowbound once all winter with a shelf full of books, including an encyclopedia. I had nothing to do but eat, sleep, and read. And I did."

"Including a stack of *Wanted* posters?" she asked slyly.

He stared at her. She returned his glance squarely, a touch of pink rising in her cheeks. He moved to the attack.

"Rimi, have you some idea I'm not just what I appear to be?"

"I do have, and I'm not sure you are," she said. "Just what, I haven't decided. I like you, Justin, and so far you have been most helpful and—and wise. One day I'll learn the truth about you. I hope the knowledge pleases me."

54

He patted her on the shoulder. "Rimi, you are a very lovely girl with an incorrigible imagination. Think what you wish of me, but you can be certain of one thing—I'm on your side, and you'll never be hurt through me."

"I suppose I'll have to be satisfied with that," she said, frowning. "Meantime, I haven't shared my imaginings with anyone else, nor will I. Now you run along and get those chores done."

An air of excitement enveloped Stoneman's Inn as the July afternoon waned. Though the windows were opened wide, there was little breeze to move the warm air laden with the succulent smell of roasting beef and ham, the tantalizing aroma of simmering soup, the pungency of onion, and the delicious aura of hot bread. Minnie Heavy Bear had learned to cook in the kitchens of the Centennial Hotel in Fort Ruskin, where all the important personages from St. Louis stopped. This day she was outdoing herself, for she was a little awed by the aristocratic Verloffs. Loyalty to Rimi Woodford made the métisse anxious to present the best of impressions.

Justin Lark was standing in the lobby chatting inconsequentially with Rimi when the front door burst open. Phil and Goldie came dashing in, their eyes wide with excitement.

"They're coming, they're coming!" Goldie cried.

"Yeah, and for gosh sakes, sis, Justin, you gotta see this!" Phil was so excited his words tumbled one over the other. "Talk about style! It's fly, I tell you, the real quill!"

Rimi and Lark hurried out onto the porch behind the two excited youngsters. The Verloff conveyance was just stopping at the foot of the steps. Lark could see why the young Woodfords were so impressed.

The horses were matched blacks, cockaded heads checkreined high, hooves polished. The vehicle was a panel-boot victoria, its top folded down, its body bright with varnish, glass lamps gleaming, wheels set off with colorful striping. On the box, in red tunics with brass buttons, white pants, and high black boots, and grand in tall silk toppers, sat a driver and footman, rigid as mannikins. In the rear seat, against the red-leather upholstery, sat a man and a woman. Lark's glance touched the man in passing, handsome, not yet to middle age, dressed to the nines. But the woman —Lark drew a deep breath of admiration. Here indeed was a beautiful creature.

Her face, perfectly oval, was framed by glossy black hair drawn taut around it. Red lips were smiling at Lark, and the dark, intense eyes seemed to burn with an inner fire.

Verloff stood, and helped his sister to her feet. The coachman held his place, staring straight ahead, but the footman stepped down and stood at attention by the side of the carriage. Without quite knowing how, Lark found himself down the steps and beside the victoria, shouldering the footman aside. He reached up for Sonya's extended hand, a long-fingered, graceful hand. She found the step with a slippered foot and stepped down, her hand in Lark's.

Lark had known some great ladies in his time, handsome women, beautiful women, but all of them had seemed to wear their clothing as a kind of personal armor, their bodies corseted tight and draped in layer upon layer of restricting cloth. Only in the privacy of their bedrooms—and sometimes not there —did they let the air and certain eyes touch lightly their naked skin. There was an exception; if fashion decreed, they displayed the beautiful bareness of shoulders, and a plunge of decolletage that emphasized the white column of throat, and the lovely swell of revealed bosom.

Sonya Verloff was dressed in that height of fashion, the bare shoulders, the long throat encircled by gold and garnets, the sweet swell of bosom. But the black satin of her gown was not armor. Somehow she lent it the impression that beneath its outer sheath there was nothing but her own sinuous body, warm and aware and promising.

Lark, holding the firm smoothness of her hand, and feeling the eyes of Rimi Woodford upon him, thought, By God, I'll do it! Bowing low over the shapely hand, he raised it to his lips. He straightened and said, "Welcome to Stoneman's Inn, Miss Verloff. I'm Justin Lark."

Her smile widened, her eyes sparkled. "Why Meestair Lark, how very continental!" she said. "I haff missed zose leetle graces in this vide, vild land."

He took her bare arm, noting the smoothness and the warmth of the ivory flesh, and led her up the steps. Sascha Verloff followed, and either because it was natural to him or to show that he was not to be outdone by Lark, bowed over the extended hand of Rimi. As young Phil held the door open, Lark heard behind them a suppressed giggle from Goldie, much amused by all this carrying-on. Rubber tires crunched softly as the victoria moved down the driveway and turned toward the rear of the inn.

"Come, Sonya, I'm sure you'd like to freshen up," Rimi said, and led her away. Lark and Verloff took seats in the parlor, on a sofa near the windows. Verloff adjusted his striped trousers, and flicked an invisible mote of dust from his polished boots. From an inner pocket he took a silver cigar case with an enameled crest. The lid came open to his thumb pressure, and he extended the case to Lark.

"Smoke, Mr. Lark? A mild claro, you'll find. I import them from Havana. Quite superior."

"Thanks, but I don't smoke," Lark said. He lied, "Lungs, you know, doctor's orders. But you go ahead."

Verloff used the gold cutter at the end of his cable watch chain to clip the cigar with all the care a surgeon uses in excising a tumor. Taking a match from a small gold matchsafe, he struck it, and with the same precise attention, he lit the Havana. He leaned back, wreathed in fragrant blue smoke, his aquiline nostrils widening to savor it. A knuckle smoothed the narrow, fine-trimmed mustache.

"You're new in this country, Mr. Lark?" he asked negligently.

"Rather," Lark said. "No doubt you heard that Clyde Prettiman had been killed. I happened along when Miss Woodford needed someone rather badly."

"You seem quite—ah, in the bosom of the family. Just what position do you hold?"

"A vague one, Verloff—sort of aide-de-camp and general factotum for Miss Woodford. She's found that a lone woman on this violent frontier—you know about

57

the recent holdup and murder—has need of some masculine muscle now and then, and perhaps an accurate gun."

"And you can supply both?" Verloff asked with an enigmatic smile.

"I can. I can claim competency in any number of directions, Verloff. The fact that my fortunes at the moment are at the nadir rather than the zenith is quite immaterial. Since they will change, they don't bother me. Pride, sir, is a thing which in certain circumstances only a fool can afford."

"But without pride a man is nothing," Verloff said, almost testily. "The pursuit of excellence, to succeed, to outwit and subdue, to be better than the next man, and the next, and the man after that, and know you are—ah, Lark, that is the most of life, aye, and the spice, too."

"Well now, I've never been bitten by a bug that makes me aspire to such ambitions," Lark said. "I take things as they come. But I won't say I disagree with you. At the moment one of my duties is driving a stage. Though some folks may consider that menial work, I take pride in doing it, and I am inclined to add a few flourishes of my own—fanfaron, you might call it."

Verloff laughed, and slapped Lark on the shoulder. "Lark, I like you. I should enlist your assistance in persuading Rimi she should sell me this inn. A time is coming when I will need this place as the key . . . ah, here come the ladies. More about that subject another time."

Later, at the table in a corner of the big dining room, there were only the six of them—Rimi Woodford and the children, Lark, and the two Verloffs. Minnie Heavy Bear, massive in a new checked gingham dress protected by a frilly white apron, served deftly. The table sparkled with snowy linen, fine china, and crystal. Rimi, at the head, seated Sascha on her right, his sister on the left. Lark held a chair for the Princess, and then for Goldie, who was seated at his left. The little girl had taken quite a shine to him. He had volunteered to give her instructions on the guitar when the time was right.

The food was excellent. As the roast was served, Verloff turned his head and called over his shoulder, "Jules! Now." To Rimi he said, "Your pardon, my dear Rimi, but I have a surprise."

The tall footman came in, minus his topper, carrying a napkin-wrapped wine bottle. He poured a dram into Verloff's crystal glass. The rancher sipped slowly, and nodded. "All right, Jules, pour. Rimi, the children can have a taste? A half-glass for them, Jules."

The footman filled the glasses with the ruby Burgundy, set the bottle on the serving table, and discreetly retired to the kitchen. Verloff raised his glass. "I would have brought a full complement of wines to please our hostess," he said, "but wine does not travel well in this heat. I felt this Beaune, to accompany our roast, was the best I could manage. It is, however, a special bottling of a vintage year."

Lark sipped his wine, and chuckled as Goldie, expecting something like soda pop or phosphate, made a face at the taste of hers. Rimi tried her glass, and said nothing. Lark sipped, frowned, and sipped again.

"Beaune, you say?" he asked Verloff. "I don't like to contradict you, sir, but this is a Pommard."

Irked, Verloff stared at him. He sipped from his own glass and put it down. He reached back to the serving table and slipped the bottle from its napkin. He read the stained label.

"By God, you're right, Lark! We brought the wrong bottle. What discrimination! I don't doubt you could tell us the year."

Lark shook his head, smiling. He had Verloff's respect now. He said, "My expertise doesn't run that deeply, but I know this is a fine wine, and must be from a fine year. And I'm pleased at your slight error, for personally I prefer the Pommard to the Beaune."

Rimi looked at him with a touch of awe. "Justin, where did you learn all that?"

He laughed. "Along the highway of my checkered career. As I told you, Rimi, I have been many places and done many things."

At the end of the meal, after cake as light and fluffy as air itself, Rimi excused the two youngsters, and brought from the inn's cellar a bottle of champagne. Lark popped the cork for her and poured the foaming golden liquid into goblets. Verloff sampled his and said, "Good. Not Veuve Clicquot, but good. Your guess, Lark."

Lark tasted it and shook his head. "This isn't a chateau pressing at all, Verloff. This is one of our premium California champagnes."

"It is? I must look into that. I did not know that they produced such excellent vintages. Sir, you have contributed to my education."

When they all moved out to the parlor, Lark found himself on a sofa sitting next to Sonya Verloff. Across from them her brother lit another of his excellent cigars. As Sonya sat close to Lark, the smooth curve of her thigh was touching his. He could feel the warmth of her flesh through the fabric. My first estimate was correct, he thought; she isn't wearing very much under that satin. But damned if I'll move away —she fascinates me.

The preliminary comments on the dinner and the weather out of the way, Sascha Verloff cleared his throat and asked, "Rimi, have you turned your thoughts toward my recent offer of purchase?"

Rimi looked at him calmly, but Lark saw her hands, folded on her lap, tighten and twist. "I have, Sascha," she said. "But I've found it too serious a thing to decide quickly. I may say yes, but give me more time, Sascha, please. If it were only myself—but it's the heritage of Phil and Goldie, too."

"Of course, of course," Verloff said. "But forty thousand dollars is a good deal of money, my dear."

"That's part of my problem, Sascha. I think your offer is too low. I know the money that was put into these buildings, I know the precision work of my father and my uncle. I'm afraid I don't consider your offer approaches the real worth of the inn."

Verloff pointed his cigar at Rimi, and Lark thought he caught a thread of exasperation in the man's voice as he said, "Sentiment, my dear Rimi, sentiment. The facts of life do not allow for sentiment. The facts of life are that the cattle market is depressed, if not destroyed. Its condition will be very bad for a long time.

60

People will tighten their belts, and stay at home. Then where will your travelers be?"

"You make a good point, Sascha. But so far my books don't give me that answer. People are still traveling, and they are still stopping at Stoneman's. It would be even better, I'm sure, if they could travel without fear of our terrible lawless element."

"Those are very bad men, I shiver when I hear vat they do," Sonya Verloff said, her throaty voice vibrant. "When I think of you at zis place alone, and maybe zose terrible men, zey come, rob you, hurt you, tear off your clothes, rape you . . ." Lark felt the little shudder where her body touched his. Why, he thought, she means this, she is afraid!

"I have those thoughts to spoil my rest," Rimi said, her voice taut. "But I love my inn. What would I do without it? Where would I go?"

"Little good it would do you if you were abused or hurt, or if some vandal put a torch to it on a dark night," Verloff said.

Lark caught the desperation in her glance. She looked at Lark for a moment, as if to draw strength from him. She said, "Sascha, I *will* give you an answer soon. But not now. You must give some thought to raising your offer; perhaps then I could make a more favorable decision."

"If that is the best you will say, I must give it more study," Verloff said, his eyes narrowed against the haze of his cigar smoke. "But the decision soon, Rimi. I want this place."

Lark said, "This seems like a far cry from ranching, Verloff. Inn-managing is a job of infinite details; the hours are long, the rewards only fair. Could you handle it?"

"That is not the problem. I would employ a competent manager, who would report to me," Verloff said rather grandly. "Then Sonya, my dear sister, could oversee the operation when I was away on business."

"But what of the lawless element? What of the Redtops?"

Verloff made an impatient gesture and stubbed out his cigar in an ashtray. "Because the ladies are fearful, we exaggerate the problem, eh, Lark? Oh, they are a nuisance, no doubt of that, and I suppose that one of these days we will have to round them up and dispose of them, once and for all."

"How do you propose to do that? Vigilante action?"

Verloff leaned back, half-smiling. "Not exactly, Lark. You admit, I'm sure, that the official law in Antelope County is a most fragile force. Not that Sheriff Looby is not a good man, but his office is undermanned, and our distances are great. That weakness can be overcome."

"I see you have given it some thought," Lark said.

"I have, and when the time comes, I'll guarantee to stamp out all vestige of crime on both sides of the Running Wolfs in a matter of a few months, even weeks. You see, Lark, I am beginning to consolidate my Rail Fence holdings. I plan to acquire, in addition to this inn, the ranches of Box B and XL and Anchor. Then I will have quite a sizable group of men at my disposal. It will be a simple matter to have every man deputized, and following a concerted plan—my plan —we will eliminate the lawless element, once and for all."

"That's a tall order," Lark said. "But when an empire is built, it must have its own army, of course."

"Exactly," Verloff said. "Lark, you are a man of deep perception. You see as I do this country needs taming; the frontier must be brushed behind us. A strong hand, Lark, that is what is needed. And that is what I, Sascha Verloff, have."

Lark said slowly, "Then after the Flats and Antelope Valley are cleaned out, there's no reason why Starr Valley should not follow in its turn. And the rest of the Territory, by the same plan—why, Verloff, the possibilities are unlimited."

"Lark, you're a man of vision!" Verloff exclaimed. "I like your attitude. As I expand, I might be able to find a place for you in my organization."

Lark nodded slowly. "I could be interested, but it would have to be something near the top. I want to be a big frog in any puddle I swim in. So if you need a competent first lieutenant, keep me in mind, Verloff."

"I will. You see, Lark, the puddle grows to a pond, and then into a lake . . ."

The front door opened, and a half-dozen people came in. Rimi stood up. "And here come our guests," she said. "Will you excuse me while I go to greet them?"

"Of course, my dear," Sonya Verloff said.

Lark stood. "You'll need me, Rimi," he said. He felt Sonya's long fingers firm and persistent on his wrist, but he pulled gently away.

As they crossed the lobby, Rimi said, with a little catch of amusement, "I see that you find the Princess quite overwhelming, Justin."

"She's utterly beautiful and completely charming," he said. "I think she scares me a little."

"Not you, Justin, not you!" she said. "And where did you pick up all that slick talk about the wine?"

He chuckled. "Don't tell the Verloffs, but I spent a year in the fine foods department of Daniels and Fisher's in Denver when I was a kid. I picked up more about gourmet foods and fine wines than you can shake a stick at."

"Well, you made an impression with it," she said. "That's what I was trying to do," he admitted. "Rimi, you were wise to stall Verloff. All the reasons for his purchase offer haven't come out, if my hunch is right."

"There have been some rumors . . ." she began, and then they were engulfed by Ted Powell, his wife, and their three pretty daughters from the XL ranch.

An hour later, when the party was in full swing, Lark watched the crowd, with the mental comment that Rimi's fiesta had stripped the country. If cattle were worth rustling, he thought, what a night this would be to build up a man's herd! But in this month of July a man couldn't give a cow away, nor a steer, nor a good Durham bull. The Big Die-Up had flooded the market with distress beef. At the moment a Montana rancher couldn't recover shipping costs to Chicago. There were wails in Boston and Edinburgh and Paris as the dismal reports of losses flooded in on the absentee owners, the great corporations which had been paying delightful profits from the beef bonanza.

And now not only their profits were wiped out, but their heavy investments as well.

He felt a small hand seek his and turned: It was Rimi's little sister, Goldie. "Justin, can we sing our song? Nearly everyone is here now."

"You bet, honey. You fetch my guitar from behind the counter while I set up our act."

He placed two chairs near the dining-room door, and when Goldie brought his guitar, he adjusted the tuning to suit him. Goldie hovered over him—a pretty child, he thought, and going to be prettier, maybe even as lovely as her big sister. Never a match for Sonya, though—look at the men hanging around her, even grouchy old Tom Fredericks. Justin, you wouldn't be a little jealous? He smiled wryly at his own conceit, but still with the hope that music might jar some of the admirers loose.

He nodded to Goldie, and swept the pick loudly across the guitar strings, and again. The room quieted. He bowed over the guitar, picking out a quick small tune. Then in a pleasing baritone he sang:

Yavapai Pete was a cowpuncher neat,
From up on the Mogollon Rim,
He lived in the saddle and punched all the cattle,
And the horse wasn't borned to throw him.

Feet began to tap and he thought, "I've got 'em!" and swung into the second verse. The crowd moved toward him, from the ladies' parlor, from the porch where couples had drifted to savor the evening coolness. Rimi had closed the taproom for the evening, but as Lark sang he noticed more than one flushed face in the audience. Some of the boys hadn't taken chances on being stranded in a desert. They had brought their own oasis.

He sang two more verses and let the music die. He said, "I could give you eight more verses, or eighty, but I'm sure you would rather hear Miss Goldie Woodford, with my assistance, sing for your pleasure, 'The Girl I Left Behind.'"

The little girl, her face taut, bowed in her best declamation manner. Lark whispered, "Loosen up, honey. They're going to love you." She gave him a shaky smile, and he struck the opening chords. Her young voice quavered a little as she began the cowboy favorite, but when Lark joined in, as they had rehearsed, her confidence returned. She picked up the verse in a true high soprano, and from that point carried the song well—so well that as they neared the end, Lark could see tears sentimental or alcoholic in the eyes of some of the listeners. Then he and Goldie brought the song to its rousing finish:

> Now when you court a pretty girl, just mark her
>   in Montan',
> For if you ride off to the southern range,
> She'll get burned with another man's brand.

Bony Cresine, one of the XL punchers, edged through the crowd. "Hey, leetle gal, that was swell! Lark, if you wouldn't mind, I could do a purty good job on 'The Streets of Laredo.'"

Without answering, Lark chorded the opening of the old cowboy classic, and backed up the grizzled old puncher as he began in a surprisingly true tenor:

> As I walked out in the streets of Laredo,
> As I walked out into old Laredo town . . .

In the arc of listeners, Lark saw Cliff Longway, a young XL puncher, watching his older sidekick. Cliff was holding Lolly Bailor's hand, and the girl, flushed and smiling, did not withdraw it. Her first party, poor kid, Lark thought. But as I predicted, she's made a conquest.

Cresine, with an instinct for showmanship, left out a number of the multitudinous verses, before the crowd might tire, and, heavily backed by Lark's guitar, came in strong on the ending:

> 'Cause I'm only a pore cowboy, and I know I done
>   wrong!

Before the wave of applause died, Lark struck up 'As I Went Walking One Morning for Pleasure,' and at its catchy beat, four couples stepped out to the center of the floor in an impromptu square dance, to the clapping of the spectators. Lark, grinning, raised the tempo, and the dancers were panting and dewed with perspiration when he swept his pick across the strings in a final chord.

He heard Rimi's voice at his ear. "That's grand, Justin. But take a break; a man has just checked in and he's asking for you. Over by the desk."

As they moved through the crowd, Sonya Verloff intercepted them. "Rimi, if you weesh, I weel play for ze entertainment."

"Oh, would you, Sonya? That would be grand," Rimi said.

"I weel send Jules to ze carriage for ze violin," she said.

The man who stood at the inn desk was weathered, solid, the outdoors plain in clothes and complexion. He said, "Justin Lark? I just rode in from Coryell. Your Aunt Susan asked me to look you up as I came through. Name's Con Tetrault."

"She's mentioned you," Lark said, shaking hands. "You here for long?"

"A few days, I guess. Depends. I may go on to Magma. Say, I didn't mean to bust in on a party."

"Miss Rimi's party; she runs the inn. Miss Woodford, that is," Lark said. "I'm sure she doesn't mind, Tetrault."

"The more the merrier," Rimi said, smiling. "Justin, will you take Mr. Tetrault and show him where to take care of his horse? Then the two of you come back and join the party."

"Yeah, I'll walk down with him and show him the ropes," Lark said. He started to lead the way toward the door, then stopped as he saw Jules, the footman, hand Sonya Verloff the violin case. He and Tetrault and Rimi stood silent as Sonya took the violin from its case, plucked the strings in adjusting the tuning, and, tucking it under her chin, raised the bow.

The first notes soared strong and sweet over the hum of party noise, and the room went silent. She swept into a melody unfamiliar to Lark, compelling in its sadness, with a throbbing ache of almost bitter yearning. At the end there was a burst of applauding, and cries of, "More! More!"

Tetrault glanced at Rimi, who was standing rapt, and said softly, "Come on, Justin, I've got to talk to you." They stepped back from the crowd and eased out the door as Sonya began the slow movement of a Hungarian *czardas,* the violin sobbing through the warm air of the room.

Outside, Tetrault untied his saddled horse and led it as he walked with Lark toward the stables. He said, in a voice touched with awe, "My God, Justin, that woman can play!"

"She can that," Lark agreed. "That's right, Con, you're a fiddler yourself."

"Call that fiddling if you want, that's concert playing," Tetrault said. "And that instrument of hers— Justin, it's worth five thousand if it's worth a cent."

Lark whistled softly. "That much? Well, it goes along with the way the Verloffs do things. Con, you bring news?"

"Some. Aunt Susan is worried. She sent me in, and Ted Collins is on his way. We've found that these Redtops have taken nearly a quarter-million in loot in the last five years. And it's almost certain the two Woodfords and Sheriff Martin were killed by them."

"I think that's right. They knew too much. Con, I'm going to send Collins on to Fort Ruskin. There's some stuff I want him to look up, county records and such. He's a regular badger when it comes to that kind of thing."

"You've got some leads?"

"Damned few, but a piece drops into place now and then. And I've got a graveyard hunch or two that might work out. I want you to go to Magma tomorrow, get next to Art Rankine, the town marshal, and Anderson, the Bear Consolidated super. Nose around a bit on the tracks of Ben Parchman, the Robbins and Tucker agent. Information leaks out of Magma, and I want to know how. Come back here Wednesday; you'll have to take over the stage run after that."

"You're dropping that cover?"

"Got to; I need more freedom, and the job's just as good cover for you. I'm making a bold move; I hope

67

it works out. But first I've got to open up to Rimi Woodford."

"Spill the whole operation? Isn't that dangerous?"

"Maybe, but she's already suspicious, and we need her cooperation, or we'll never break this thing open. She's smart, and discreet. She'll play along."

"All right, I'll move on to Magma tomorrow. And what will happen when I get back Wednesday?"

Lark said grimly, "On Wednesday, when I get back with the shuttle from Magma, right in front of God and everybody, Miss Rimi Woodford and I are going to have one hell of a fight."

7

Stoneman's Gap, M.T.
July 5, 1887

Dear Aunt Susan:

Your friend Mr. Tetrault is visiting Magma, will be back Wednesday. Hope to see your friend Mr. Collins soon on his way to Fort Ruskin.

I am changing location soon, and mail may be slow. Mr. Tetrault will be in touch, as I intend to accept an invitation to visit at the Rail Fence Ranch with the Verloffs.

Have you heard anything from Uncle Allan in Chicago? You know my interest in European politics, so be sure to ask him about the Polish situation.

Your aff. nephew,
Justin

Lark stood massaging the taut muscles of his neck as the heavily loaded stage wagon rattled off toward Magma. Phil Woodford's first swing of the whip was abortive, but the second try brought a highly satisfactory crack in the best stage-driver style. Besides Lark, Rimi Woodford waved her handkerchief in farewell. She seemed a bit worried about the two young ones going off alone, but had not the heart to forbid them the exciting celebration of the Fourth at Magma.

The stage wagon rattled out of sight around the bend. Its complement was nine passengers inside, with Goldie Woodford and Nancy Powell beside Phil on the box; the other two Powell girls and Dorrie Abel from Anchor on the stage-top seats above the box. And there were outriders, Bony Cresine and Cliff Longway from XL, Jim Warner from Anchor, Dazzy Furlong from Star Cross, and Con Tetrault. Lark noted that there were no Rail Fence punchers among the fun-seeking riders. Verloff must keep his employees on a tight checkrein of discipline.

As they went back into the coolness of the inn, Rimi said, "Oh, dear! I hope they have fun, but I'm afraid of trouble. It will be pretty wild in Magma."

"It could be," Lark said. They sat down on a sofa near the window. The parlor was neat, for a willing crew had cleaned up last night's disorder as the price of going to Magma. Now there was only the rattle of dishes and the clink of silver as Minnie Heavy Bear and Lolly Bailor finished the chores from the midnight supper.

Lark leaned back, stretching his booted feet in front of him. "I wouldn't worry though, young lady. I asked Tetrault to keep an eye on them, and Art Rankine won't let anything very violent get going; he'll bust it up in a hurry. Lots of other kids there, too; ours should have a ball. So quit worrying."

Rimi put a hand on Lark's knee. "I'll try not to, Justin. But I have other worries. Like why you lied to me."

"Lied to you? How's that?"

"To an experienced hotel keeper like myself, there are little signs which tell volumes. You're an excellent actor, Justin, but not good enough to conceal the fact that you already knew Con Tetrault. And I don't like it."

He covered her work-roughened hand with his large callused palm. "Rimi, you're a sweet girl, and you're smart. Maybe too smart for your own good. I see where you and I have got to make medicine, big medicine. And when you've heard me out you can either call for cards or throw in your hand. Will you take a walk with me this afternoon?"

"My, you do sound mysterious, Justin. But that's only one of the mysteries which bother me. Of course I'll go. Say two o'clock? I've got a pile of paperwork I must get done while the inn is empty and there are no stages coming and going. Tomorrow the carrousel will start all over again.",

"Two o'clock it is. That will give me an hour or two to spark Miss Lolita Bailor when she gets through in the kitchen."

Rimi stared at him. "Justin Lark, that child! I know she's crazy about you, with those big eyes she watches every move you make. She goes breathless when she talks about you. But honestly . . ."

"Why Rimi, you know I love that redhead! She's pretty and healthy, and a man could train her to be a fine, obedient mate, and Minnie is already teaching her to cook. I'll admit she's young, all of five or six years younger than the old crones of your generation."

She recognized his bantering tone, but did not know exactly how to interpret it. "Justin, I'm sure you do love her, but so do I. You wouldn't hurt her, would you?"

Reaching out, he patted Rimi's cheek and watched the color flame in the girl's face. "You know I wouldn't," he said gently. "All her thoughts of old man Lark, in the mists of memory in years to come, will be kindly ones, I hope. Already she's about to fall head over heels in love with a promising young cowhand named Cliff Longway, who will no doubt end up as a successful rancher and a member of the legislature. But meantime, old man Lark is going to softsoap that pretty little thing until she tells him everything she knows or suspects about the Bailors and the Sumters and the Prettimans."

Rimi's breath drew in sharply. "But why, Justin? What connection is there . . . ?"

"The why you'll learn this afternoon when I spark *you*," he said, with a grin. He released her hand and stood up. "As for what Lolly knows, it may be much, it may be little. She may not even know she knows it. But I've got to have background, so bear with me, my dear. If I wasn't already sure how close you can keep your pretty mouth clam-tight shut, I wouldn't have told you this much. We may be talking literally about life and death."

"You frighten me, Justin," she whispered.

"I intended to," he said cheerfully. "But one reason I am here is to keep people from getting hurt. Run along, now."

When she had gone to her bookwork, Lark stretched out against the back of the sofa, lulled by the slight sounds of the inn. The dull headache engendered by last night's mild overindulgence faded away in the peace and quiet of the warm July morning. He relaxed, though he still wondered if he was being wise in opening this circle of dangerous knowledge to Rimi Woodford. But he could see no other course. She had become a key figure.

Last night, when Tetrault's mount had been fed and watered and bedded down, the two men had walked back toward the inn. It was full dark except for the blaze of a myriad stars, and the friendly lamplight of the inn. Through the open windows soared the haunting music of Sonya Verloff's violin, crying, talking, and as they came into the lobby, reaching up the scale to end on a note so high it was almost inaudible. The applause went on and on.

Finally Sonya raised her bow for silence. "I thank you, my friends, you are very kind. But I know you want to dance, and I do not know, what you call, ze country music. If anyone here, they can ze violin play . . ." She held out the bow toward them.

Lark nudged Tetrault in the ribs with an elbow. "There you go, Con. You've been itching to get your hands on that fiddle."

Tetrault elbowed his way through the press and stepped up beside Sonya. She gave him the violin, and watched a little anxiously while he tucked the rest under his chin. But he had played only a few strutting notes of "Buffalo Gals" when she smiled, nodded in satisfaction, and moved out from the crowd. They were forming sets when she found Lark, tucked her hand under his arm, and led him out to the coolness of the porch.

"Your friend, he plays goot," she said. "I know when he puts his chin down he knows ze fine instrument, he weel shoot his mother before he weel put even a leetle scratch on ze varnish of such a violin. So we let him play, eh? Eet is hot in there, and maybe I have a leetle bit too much of ze wine."

"Something makes your eyes sparkle, but I was hoping it was the company," Lark said. He sat on the porch railing, watching as she leaned against a pillar, black and white of gown and shoulders against the stark white of the pillar. Deliberate or not, her pose was graceful to the point of enticement. He said, "You seem a creature of the cities, Sonya. I see you under the bright lights of fine parties, involved in international comings and goings. What are you doing on a rough Montana ranch? Do you enjoy it?"

She laughed and took his hand in hers, her long tapering fingers warm and trusting. "Justin, those cities in Europe, zey are fine for the people of money, with ze great fortunes, ze rich jewels and ze palaces. But for others, not so goot. Owning a fortune, zat is easy, just be born to eet. But to make a fortune, zat is *très difficile,* maybe impossible. In America, on ze frontier, ees not so hard. A man like Sascha, a woman like me, we take our talents and our wits and we build ze fortune for ourselves. Oh, eet take much planning and sacrifice and hard work. But eet can be done—we are doing eet. Later weel come ze travel, ze parties, ze fine life. Now I put up with ze weather and ze loneliness and ze discomfort, and look ahead to better times."

"A good philosophy," Lark said. "And how near is your goal?"

"Still far, I am afraid. Ze land, Sascha says zat is ze key. Already he has ranch ver' large. Eet weel grow bigger, as other ranchers are—w'at you say, discouraged?—by their winter losses; some weel sell out sheap. And Stoneman's Gap, zat he weel acquire also, eet is of value when comes through here ze . . ."

"Sonya, you will catch yourself a cold, my dear."

72

The suave voice of Sascha Verloff was not peremptory, but there was an edge of force in it. "Come inside, my dear; I am sure Mr. Lark will excuse you. You should listen to the young man who is using your violin. He plays well, very well."

Sonya straightened, making a little moue of annoyance. Lark slid his hip from the railing. "That's OK, Verloff," he said. "I was going to bring her in anyhow. I should lend the music of my guitar to the dancing."

As he dropped the strap of his guitar around his neck, Lark was still mulling over Sonya's last statement. The involuted phrases in her Polish accent made it hard for him to guess at what she had been about to say. It would seem that she shared to some extent the ambitions of her brother, and did what she could to further those long-range plans.

Late in the evening one of the Rail Fence riders had a minor altercation with Cliff Longway, over the favors of Lolly Bailor. Lark was amused to see how quickly a single sharp word from Verloff ended it. Discipline, Lark thought, iron discipline, the old-country way. A cowpoke is usually as independent as a hog headed for the wars. Wonder how Verloff makes 'em like it?

It was midnight when the Verloffs made their good-byes to Rimi Woodford, pleading the long drive back to Rail Fence. With reluctance, Con Tetrault cased Sonya's violin and carried it as with Rimi and Lark he escorted Sonya and her brother to the waiting victoria. Lark handed Sonya up into the vehicle, and Tetrault reached the violin case in to her.

"A fine fiddle, Miss Verloff, very fine," he said. "I appreciated the chance to play it."

"You mus' come to Rail Fence and play heem some more," she said, smiling. "Eh, Sascha? And you come too, Rimi, and you, Justin. Stay for a day or for a week; we wish to show you our new house, our fine land. You weel come, please?"

Rimi smiled without answering. Lark said, "I'll take you up on that one day soon, Sonya. Be seeing you."

"Always welcome, Lark, always welcome," Sascha Verloff said. "Rimi, thank you again. And let me have your word soon on our little matter, eh?" To the driver:

"Pendergast, let us be on our way." He sank back into the red-leather upholstery beside his sister as the four Rail Fence riders moved out ahead of the carriage. The coachman, with Jules sitting rigid, arms folded, beside him, touched the blacks with the tip of the switch, and the rig rolled smartly away. The folded top of the victoria had been raised against the night chill, so Lark had only a glimpse of a waved handkerchief as the carriage spun off toward Rail Fence, sixteen miles to the north. He watched the lighted carriage lamps disappear into the night and thought—how aristocratic! Or, as Sonya had said—how very continental!

Now in the quiet of the inn, Lark leaned back, eyes closed, trying to recall exactly all Verloff had said. He thought he could sense the beginning of a pattern, certainly too vague even to mull over with Tetrault, but one he had observed before, in Colorado, in New Mexico, in Oregon. A man making the big gamble, Lark thought, and shook his head. Not recognizing the anachronism, a man tries to grasp and dominate and subdue as the lords of the castle did in feudal times. Such plans were foredoomed to failure, but before they failed, before they were thwarted, good men and good women would suffer cruelly. That's the hell of it, Lark thought.

He rubbed a palm thoughtfully along his jaw. If he were on the right track, then he could chart the solution. The steps he had already taken, though taken in the dark, were in the right direction. With Tetrault here and Collins assigned, he would soon determine what course to pursue. He could be wrong, of course.

His musings were interrupted by the sound of footsteps and he looked up to see Lolly Bailor crossing the room. He stood up as she approached.

"Miss Rimi said you wanted to see me," she said shyly.

"I do. Lolly, did you have a good time last night?"

"Mr. Lark, it was wonderful!" she said. "All the people, and the music and dancing and all. Cliff—Mr. Longway—he saw I had a good time and even showed me how to dance."

"I noticed Cliff didn't stray far from your vicinity,"

74

Lark said. Pink rose in the girl's cheeks. "He's a darned nice fellow," he added. "Lolly, how about taking a walk with me?"

"Why, that sounds nice," she said. "Down by the river?"

"It's pleasant there. Let's go," he said, taking her arm.

They walked along the main road, and beyond the wagon yard turned into a path that crossed a meadow starred with early summer flowers, leading toward the Redstone. They found a fallen tree along the bank and took a seat on this natural bench. Below them, the Redstone was high in its banks, its waters yellowed by silt, hissing and splashing with snow melt and the last of the spring rains. It seemed to hurry toward the dark cleft of Dead Man's Canyon.

Across the meadow and the road, Lark could see the inn, set among the trees. It looks like a building transplanted from New England, he thought. But the harsh and menacing peaks behind the inn have small resemblance to the rounded hills and gentle valleys of that distant region. And life must be more tamed and serene than it is here at Stoneman's Gap.

"Are you happy here, Lolly?" he asked.

"Oh, Mr. Lark, it's like—like a new life!" she said with a quick intake of breath. "It's so heavenly I keep thinking—well, something or somebody will ruin it for me."

"Your family, you mean? Your brothers?"

"Them, maybe, or some other shiftless relations. They'd do it too, Mr. Lark, if only for pure meanness. And they will." There was a note of hopelessness in her fresh young voice. "I've had to take that all my life, Mr. Lark, so I guess I can still take it. What worries me is that I might bring trouble on Miss Rimi, just because she helped me."

"We'll have to try to see that they don't. If I knew more about them—Lolly, why do you fear your own family so much?"

"Because they're bad, Mr. Lark. They're evil. All of them but Marsh, and two or three of the Prettimans or Sumters. My father, Billy Bailor, is old before his time, a sneaking, conniving old skunk. My other brothers are just as mean and crooked and full of hell. The Bailors have good land on Box B, but do they work it? Oh no, they're too lazy for that. They'd sooner make one crooked dollar than a hundred clean ones. I'm not a saint, Mr. Lark, but I try to be decent. But my family—they just seem to enjoy filth and rottenness."

"A lovely bunch," Lark commented. "No wonder you ran away from them. What kind of crookedness were they mixed up in, Lolly?"

"I don't know. I didn't want to know. Sometimes they'd be gone for a spell and when they came back they'd have money. They'd give a little to Paw and then they'd take off for Fort Ruskin or Copperton or Coryell. When they came back they'd keep bragging about the big times they had, about the—the redlight houses and the fancy women. It never bothered them to talk like that right in front of me. It fair made me sick."

"Lolly, I don't like to say this, but it could be that your brothers are mixed up in the Redtop gang."

She nodded. "I've thought of that, too. Tom Towe, the one that got hisself killed in a holdup a while back, he was married to a Sumter girl, my ma's folks. But there's a couple of things that bother me about that, Mr. Lark. My brothers ain't very brave, and they ain't very smart. I don't think they got the gall nor the smart to keep on robbing stages and freighters and travelers for such a long time and not get caught. Then, I heard some of those robberies was big ones. Well, the boys had money, but never the kind of money they would have got from those, thousands and thousands of dollars."

"Maybe they were hired hands for a third party."

"That might be it," she said slowly. "For somebody with brains to tell the fools what to do . . . I do know one thing, Mr. Lark, they wasn't in on that Magma bank holdup, when Mr. Rankine got hurt. The bunch of 'em happened to be home, and when Pike Sumter came riding in with the news, all of 'em were mad enough to spit. Anse swore something awful. He says, 'We been left holding the tarred end of the stick again.' Pike laughed at him and says, 'That was one hell of a

76

smooth operation. Mebbe the Man was scairt you'd gum up the works.' Anse just about drew down on Pike, but Pike's a pretty tough customer hisself, and he just laughed at Anse until Anse calmed down."

"Interesting," Lark said. He picked up a broken stick and traced idle patterns in the soft black dirt. "Never a word came to your ears, Lolly, as to who the Man might be? The Man who was in the market for hired guns?"

She shook her head. "No, and I tried not to listen. I was scairt enough without knowing any secrets. Nor it weren't safe—a day or so before he got killed, Tom Towe rode out to Box B. They was all drinking and arguing and I went outside. After a while Tom come out and climbed on his horse, pretty drunk. He yelled, 'All right, I'll do it myself. Alone. And I'll keep it all. You want in, come to the Slot next Tuesday. But you're too damn scairt!' and he rode away. Then I heard Anse say, 'The Man ain't gonna like this. Maybe he ought to know.' A while later I saw Lippy ride out. He was gone for a few days. Next we heard, Percy had been ready, and when Tom stepped out of the brush and says 'Hands up!' Percy blew him in two with the shotgun."

Lark stood up. "Little Lolly, you're well out of that horrible mess. Listen, if any of those boys bother you a single minute, let me know. If I'm not here, tell Mr. Tetrault. And Lolly, you will see and hear things in the next few days that will shake you up. Just remember that you don't always see what you think you see, nor hear what you think you hear. Come on, Rusty, let's get on back."

8

Stoneman's Gap, M.T.
July 6, 1887

Dear Aunt Susan:

Your friend Mr. Collins came in late yesterday; we had a nice chat. He furnished me the historical data Uncle Allan sent from Chicago. Find it interesting, gives me a new slant. Indications are now the Polish situation could develop into the key of the puzzle. So I am going to Rail Fence to visit a few days, may pin something down.

If anything should develop on File 262 (the number given me by Mr. Collins) refer it to Mr. Tetrault, or if he is not there, reach Miss Woodford, who is now au courant with File 262. She is completely reliable. Do not have a tizzy about this, auntie, it had to be done.

Your aff. nephew,
Justin

‹‹‹‹‹‹‹‹‹‹‹‹‹‹‹‹‹‹‹‹‹‹‹‹‹‹‹‹‹‹‹

"Did our Lolly have anything new to tell you?" Rimi asked, an odd edge of coolness in her voice.

"She had a wonderful time last night—the inn is heaven and you are its superior angel—her starry-eyed affection is now transferred to one Cliff Longway, an XL puncher younger and more handsome than me." Lark flipped a pebble over the brink toward the roof of the inn below them, and turned to grin at Rimi.

High on the hillside at the back of the inn, they were sitting on the edge of the wooden cover which fitted over the round masonry wall enclosing the spring. From the base of the wall, the water-supply pipe led over the lip of the ledge and down to the inn. The pipe was enclosed in a wooden cover filled with sawdust. This spring never slackened or changed temperature, Rimi had told Lark. It would furnish many times the demands of the inn and its apartment buildings for water.

"That's new?" Rimi asked dryly, but the coolness was gone from her voice. "Woman's intuition had told me that much."

Lark reached over and took her hand. She did not resist, but looked at him and then away, a slight flush rising in cheeks touched with the gold of the summer sun. He turned the hand over, noting the thickened skin of hard-worn calluses. Never the silken smoothness of Sonya's hands, he thought. This girl works hard, and has, all her life.

"Rimi, the time has come to sweep away your doubts and suspicions with the broom of truth," he said. "I said you were a smart girl; your analysis of me proves that—it was correct. I'm not what I pretended to be. In my life I've done many things, but for a long time I've earned my living as an investigator for the Pinkerton National Detective Agency, working out of the Denver office."

"And you're here on the trail of the Redtop gang?" She did not show great surprise, although the hand he was holding closed suddenly over his fingers.

"Originally. We were called in by your Robbins and Tucker Stage Lines. Their losses were getting completely out of the range of tolerance. Now things seem to be going beyond mere robbery, beyond the Redtops. And you were right, too, about Con Tetrault; he's not only an old and valued friend, but a fellow Pinkerton operative as well. We have word now that additional clients have joined the case—Bear Consolidated at Magma, and Brant-Lochray Metals at Copperton. They've both had severe losses. Now there's a new client—hold your breath, young lady—Preston H. Leslie, governor of the Territory of Montana."

"The governor!" Rimi exclaimed, startled.

"No less. Seems that the ranchers of the Padlock and

79

Starr valleys sent the governor a petition asking for something drastic to be done against the wave of robberies and murders. There aren't enough U.S. marshals to put a dent in this big a ring, and the few we have are overworked. So Governor Leslie got in touch with Allan Pinkerton in Chicago. The governor was surprised to learn that there were already Pinkerton operatives on the case. Mr. Pinkerton warned Governor Leslie not to mention to anyone that we are involved, but it's only a matter of time before some word leaks out. So we've got to move at high speed."

"That petition, I remember it now," Rimi said. "Ted Powell told me he had signed it. Didn't think it would do much good."

"He did sign, and Fredericks, and even our friend Verloff. We've been handed something, Rimi; that's why I'll need your cooperation. The shadow of this lawlessness grows longer all the time. And Stoneman's Gap is right square in the middle of it. I hate to involve you . . ."

Smiling, she closed her hand tight on his. "Justin, I'm already involved. I'm praying for the end of this terror by day and night. And while it may be un-Christian, and bitter, and wicked, I've got to see that the men who killed my father and uncle pay for their crimes. Justin, the heartlessness of that, the cruelty . . ." Her voice broke, and she covered her face with her hands, to screen out the shocking memory of it.

Lark put a consoling hand on her shoulder. "We'll present a bill, and not rest until it's marked PAID IN FULL. Remember, Rimi, our agency has a long record of success in breaking up criminal conspiracies, and bringing the guilty to justice. The Pinkertons broke up the Molly Maguires, for instance, and those Irishmen were tougher and more bloodthirsty than even the Redtops can think of being. Oh, it won't be easy, and people will get hurt, but in the end we'll scotch them for good."

"But Justin, it's so well-covered, so secret! Do you have any suspicions?"

He looked into those blue eyes and nodded. "Things are beginning to fit together. But that's all I'm going to tell you right now, young lady, only as much as you need to know. It's dangerous for you, from now on, to even hint that you ever heard of the Pinkerton Agency. If there's an emergency, get in touch with Con. Because I won't be here—listen closely now, this is what I want you to do . . ."

The mud wagon came hurtling down the main road toward Stoneman's Gap at a breakneck pace. In the heat of the late afternoon, a dust cloud swirled high behind the racing stage and spiraled toward the blue bowl of the sky. The driver, feet braced against the footrest, was urging the horses on with shouts and cracking whip.

The stage took the turn into the driveway, teetering up on two wheels precariously, then settling level with a jar. The driver braced, hauling back on the reins, riding the brake pedal hard. With brakeblocks screeching, the stage jolted to a halt at the inn steps, a yellow-gray billow of dust catching up with it, half blinding Rimi Woodford, who was watching from the porch of the inn.

Lark wrapped the lines around the whip socket and swung down from the box. He lurched as his boots hit the gravel, and he steadied himself with a hand on the heaving flank of the off wheeler. He saw Rimi on the porch, and with a whoop he went up the steps two at a time. He grabbed the girl, and like a clumsy bear, waltzed her around and around.

"Justin, stop it!" she cried, not amused. "What on earth do you think you're doing?"

"A man has to turn his wolf loose once in a while, pretty lady," Lark cried. "I didn't have any passengers from Magma, so I thought I'd set a record for the run. Damn near did, too."

"You didn't do our two teams any good," she said pointedly. Noting that half a dozen overnight guests, who were sitting in the cool of the porch, were showing interest, she lowered her voice. "Justin, you've been drinking."

"So I have, so I have," Lark said loudly. "You wouldn't let me go to Magma for the Glorious Fourth, so'm celebrating it today."

81

"All right, all right, go and get those horses taken care of," she said, her voice angry. "Where's the mail sack?"

He looked at her blankly, then a slow smile dawned on his face. He leaned back against a porch pillar. "Well, don't that beat all? I plumb forgot to pick the dang thing up!"

She stared at him, her eyes flashing. At that moment a horseman rode up behind the stage. He swung down from his mount and came up the steps. He handed a mail sack to Rimi.

"Your driver forgot this, miss," Con Tetrault said. "And on top of that, he tore down the road from Magma like a crazy man. Wonder he didn't kill your horses and himself both. Not that he would have been any great loss."

Lark's bantering mood turned ugly. A snarl in his voice, his words slurring a little, he said, "So Mister Biggety, you're saying I can't drive stage. What you trying to do, run me off so you can get my job?"

"I sure as hell could do a better job than you did today," Tetrault said.

Lark took one lurching step and hit him. Tetrault staggered back, his shoulders banging against the wall of the inn. His hat fell off, but he didn't bother to retrieve it as he started for Lark.

Rimi Woodford stepped between them. "Stop it, you men! Justin, that's the last straw! I can't put up with this any longer; you're fired. Get your stuff and get out of here, right now. Mr. Tetrault will unharness and put up the teams, won't you, Mr. Tetrault?"

"Damn right I will, and I'll drive it for you tomorrow, too," Tetrault said. "You going to make this ranny walk away?"

"There's a saddle mule in the corral and an old hull in the bar. You take that beast, Justin, and ride out. You and the mule will make a good pair—you're both stubborn and mean."

Lark laughed loudly without amusement. "So we've gone high and mighty now, eh? Well, you weren't so damn finicky t'other night when we . . ."

Her hand came around in a full arc and took him across the face with an angry splat. He stared at her

82

stupidly, shoulders slumped, rubbing his cheek. Then he turned, jerked open the screen door, and disappeared into the inn.

There were tears in Rimi's eyes and a catch in her voice as she spoke to the hotel patrons who had been watching. "I'm sorry, folks, for this unpleasantness. But I am *not* going to stand for that kind of insolence from one of my employees. Please forgive us, and I ask that you don't let it spoil your stay at Stoneman's Inn."

Lark came through the door, carrying a canvas sack bulging with his belongings, and Rimi stepped aside. Before she could escape, Lark dropped the sack and swept her into his arms. She cried out as he bent her back and kissed her hard and long. Tetrault, hard-eyed and with an air of competence, stepped forward and laid a heavy hand on Lark's shoulder. He jerked him away. "That will be enough of that, mister," he said coldly. "You let this little lady alone and get out of here." His hand dropped toward the holstered pistol at his thigh.

"Oh, okay, okay," Lark grumbled. "But you'll regret this, Miss Rimi Woodford. I'll be back one day soon and settle accounts with you."

"Your wages so far won't offset the advance I made you, plus your meals," Rimi said. "But I'll call that square, just to be rid of you. Now get!"

Lark picked up his duffel bag. He lurched down the steps and took an erratic course toward the stables. A few minutes later the onlookers saw Lark ride out on a big gray mule, guitar case and duffel sack tied behind the saddle. He turned west on the Fort Ruskin road without a backward glance. Rimi, watching, gave a muffled sob and ran blindly into the inn, the screen door banging shut behind her.

At the Y where the Copperton and Fort Ruskin roads split, Lark turned the mule north. He was grinning, savoring the scene just played. Why, you might do well treading the boards, Justin, he told himself. He put his left hand, fingers spread, against his chest and declaimed, "Shall we buy treason? and indent with fears, when they have lost and forfeited themselves? No, on the barren mountains let him starve, for I shall never hold that man my friend . . ." I could do King Henry like a damn, I betcha. Old Con wasn't bad, either—when he faked that bounce against the wall everybody thought I'd knocked the old boy's head half off. And Rimi—that was a star performance, the quivering voice, the tears, the hot show of anger —a good job, mighty good. Only, when I kissed her, those sweet lips answered mine, I'll swear it. That wasn't in the script. Now there's no time for love or thoughts of love, but when this is all wound up in a tight ball, we'll see, we'll see. If I'm still alive, that is. . . .

The sun was slanting low over the crown of the Padlocks when Lark stopped Mingus, the mule, at the lane leading from the highway to Rail Fence. An arched gateway of mortared stone, with a double gate of wrought iron, was topped by the XXX emblem of Rail Fence, done in twisted iron. The elegance of the gateway was diluted somewhat by the fact that the masonry wings extended north and south only ten feet, then joined a more plebeian fence of three strands of barbed wire stretched tautly on cedar posts.

Lark opened the gate, rode through, and closed it behind him. Down the lane he could see, perhaps a quarter-mile away among trees, a big house of two stories. As he neared it he was surprised to see how big it was, almost half the size of Stoneman's Inn. It was set against the rise of a hill. Lark rode his mule up to a large red barn, well away from the house.

Beyond the barn was a low building, with a porch extending all along one side—the bunkhouse, no doubt, as half a dozen of the hands were sitting in the shadow. They were smoking, working on clothing or lass' ropes, or just dozing in the July heat. As Lark swung down, a door in the end of a dwelling nearer the ranch house opened, and a man came out. He strode across the yard toward Lark.

"What d'you think you're doing here, pilgrim?" he demanded.

Lark looked at him. For a fleeting scrap of a second, he felt he knew this man from somewhere, then the impression vanished. The man stood tautly, a tall man, craggy of feature, weather-worn, heavy of mustache and hard of eye.

"Name's Lark," he said. He extended a hand, but the man ignored it. "I came here on the invitation of Miss Verloff. You tell her I'm here, eh?"

"Lark, huh? You the guy was drivin' the Magma stage?"

"Yeah, but I quit. The Woodford woman is too bossy for me. Thought I'd come over here and spend a few days."

"Mister, Miss Verloff don't waste her time on saddle tramps. So why don't you hop back on that mangy critter of yours and git to hell out of here?" The man made no motion toward the six-gun strapped at his hip, but somehow he gave Lark notice of it.

Lark smiled at him. "You must not have heard me. I'm here at the personal invitation of Miss Verloff. So run along, fellow, stir your stumps and tell her that I'm here."

"Why, you son-of-a-bitch!" the man growled, and his hand dropped toward the butt of his gun. And in the next ten seconds Lark, with that deceptive speed of his, destroyed the man. He took one step and kneed the man in the crotch, and seizing the gun hand, turned and levered the man over his shoulder. The body hit the ground heavily, Lark stamped a heel hard on the gun wrist, and put the toe of the other boot hard into the pit of the man's stomach. The remaining air in the man's lungs drove out with a whoosh.

Lark reached over the inert body and picked up the pistol. He shucked out the shells and tossed them aside. Then he flipped the empty gun half across the yard. The watchers on the porch had come storming down and formed a half-circle around Lark. He looked at them with a taut smile.

"Sorry to do this, fellows, but this bird was pushing me," he said. "Who is he?"

"Rod Starbolt, the foreman," a puncher said, grudging respect in his voice.

"For some reason he objected when I asked him to tell Miss Verloff that her guest was here," Lark said. "You can see, boys, I don't much stand for objections."

"You got a hell of a nerve, mister," another puncher said. Lark noticed that the middle finger of the man's right hand was missing, yet his denims were worn smooth at holster height on his right side. Carries his six-gun for a cross draw, Lark thought. Something familiar about that—and he filed it away in the back of his mind.

"Damn right I have," Lark said pleasantly. "Now one of you run up to the house and tell Miss Verloff I'm here."

The man with the missing finger stood still, but the slim puncher who had spoken first grinned and started toward the big house in the rolling clumsy stride of the cowboy in high-heeled boots. The others held their ground, arced about Lark like wolves around an old buffalo bull.

On the ground, Starbolt was groaning, his knees drawn up to his middle. His hands went to his groin and he rolled over on his side, his face pale, his eyes closed, moaning in short rhythmic bursts. One of the men started to assist him, but Lark said sharply, "No!" and the man stopped in his tracks.

The door of the big house opened, and the slim puncher came hurrying out, followed by Sascha Verloff. When the punchers saw their employer, they all eased away except the man with the maimed hand. They were back on the bunkhouse porch by the time Verloff reached the downed Starbolt.

"Your work, Lark?" Verloff snapped, sounding annoyed but not deeply angry. He nudged the injured man with a boot toe.

"My work," Lark said. "He took umbrage at my presence and tried to run me off the place, though I told him I was here by your invitation. I don't go for that, Verloff. Next time he takes matters into his own hands, I'm afraid I'll have to kill him."

Verloff stared at Lark, frowning. Then he smiled. "I believe you would, at that. I've got to hand it to you, Lark. My man Starbolt here has a reputation as a tough cookie, but you cut him down to size. Bailor, you and the others get Starbolt back to his house so Amy can take care of him. Slim, see that Mr. Lark's mule is taken care of. Lark, grab your baggage and come along with me."

Bailor signaled, and one of the other men came back. Between the two of them they got the agonized Starbolt to his feet, as Slim led the Mingus mule away. The two men half-walked, half-dragged Starbolt toward his quarters, his knees still convulsively bent, his body sagged in a bow. As the trio moved away, Lark saw that it was the man with the missing finger Verloff had called Bailor. Lippy Bailor, then, and the maimed hand was a souvenir of the Bailors' encounter a few years ago with old Willis Stoneman and his .30-30.

Carrying his duffel bag and guitar case, Lark followed Verloff across the yard and up the steps of the big house.

"You're not very stylishly mounted, Lark," Verloff observed.

Lark laughed. "The mule, you mean? It's quite a story. I got so damn tired of the routine of driving stage, I got drunk in Magma. I'm not a drinking man, and this was the first toot in years, but it was a good one. I drove the stage back too fast to suit Miss Rimi, and she fired me. Which I guess was what I wanted —she's pretty mad at me, but I'm sure she'll get over it."

Verloff held the door open for him. "But how did you happen to come here, to Rail Fence?"

"I'll be honest with you, Verloff," Lark said. "I feel that I'm cut out for bigger things than driving a four-horse hitch, much bigger. So I've been thinking about that tentative offer you made the other night. I might be willing to dicker, if the terms look right."

Verloff did not answer as he led the way into a wide hall. From it a staircase rose in a graceful curve toward the upper floors. From across the hall came the sound of piano music, well played, Lark thought; Sonya, of course. The two men stood quiet while the music soared to a triumphant crescendo, and died in the crash of a chord.

Verloff said to the little maid, crisp in black and white, who appeared almost magically, "Marie, this is Mr. Lark. Take his things up to—yes, the blue room. Come, Lark, Sonya is in the music room."

They crossed the large parlor to the smaller music room beyond. The rooms were ornately papered, with dark drapes over fine lace curtains on the tall windows. *Objets d'art* were everywhere, gilt mirrors, glass and ormolu, Dresden china, carved sconces and crystal chandeliers. Stern ancestral faces peered down from heavy gilt frames on the walls. The floors were covered with deep-piled carpet, and at the side of the parlor was a great tiled fireplace with a marble mantel.

Sonya Verloff smiled at them from the bench in front of the rosewood grand piano. She stood up and came to Lark, both hands extended. "Why, Meestair Lark, how fine to see you again so soon. You will, I hope, stay with us a few days at least?"

Again Lark found something electric in the touch of her hands. "I hope so," he said. "But it's more or less up to your brother."

"As a matter of face, my dear, Lark may take a position with my organization," Verloff said.

"You haff left the employ of Rimi, then? There ees a luffly child, though somewhat *moujik*—wa't you say, proletarian?—*gauche*, perhaps. If she weel sell Sascha ze inn, she would have money for ze study, ze travel —but enough of my friend Rimi. I am happy, Meestair Lark—Justin—that you may join forces with my brother. You would learn much from his genius."

Was there a faint hint of irony in her voice? Lark wondered. Reluctantly he released her hands. "I guess I could. I like his style; he's the kind of man who gets things done, and so am I. We'd make a team. Say, I heard you playing as we came in. You play piano as well as you do violin, and that's very very well."

"Thank you, Justin, but I do not play either as well as I should, for I do not practice as one must to be ze really good musician. I play mostly for my own amusement and Sascha's. But if you stay, I will play for you also."

"I'll be looking forward to that," Lark said. "Now if you don't mind, I'll get cleaned up a little. I smell too much of sweat and horse to be a fit guest in such a beautiful house."

She laughed. "You have only ze universal smell of this rough country, *n'est-ce pas?* But you go up, Marie will show you your room, also ze bathroom. We do not dine in style tonight, Justin, only a small snack in ze kitchen."

When he returned, well-scrubbed and in a clean shirt, she was waiting for him. He looked at her admiringly. Though she was dressed in a simple cotton check, the utilitarian dress could not conceal that sinuous and exciting litheness of hers. As he followed her to the kitchen, he said, "I like your house."

"Eet is beautiful, no? Though eet is not yet—how you say it?—half-baked? No, no, I mean eet is not half done. We haff plans that weel make eet ze showplace of Montana."

The big kitchen with its tiled cooking area had a pleasantly old-world charm. The dining nook looked out over the ranch yard, and through the windows the walls were painted by the flaming plumes of the sunset. Lark found the meal good, and being hungry, did full justice to it. The buxom cook, who had also served, placed a creamy dessert in front of each of them and discreetly withdrew.

Through eating, Verloff took out his silver case, and selected and lit a cigar. He started to reach the case toward Lark, then stopped. "Oh, I forgot. Your lungs, you said?"

"Yes, brought me out west as a boy, for my health and to seek my fortune," Lark said. "My health has improved more than my fortune. I had the key once, but I lost it. I'm looking for it again, and I won't give up until I find it. Or die, one."

Verloff regarded him through a curling wreath of cigar smoke. He said to Sonya, "My dear, after we have enjoyed a glass of port, why don't you busy yourself with something, while Lark and I talk business?"

"I find business ver' dull, as you know, dear brother," she said. "I was hoping you would absolve me of ze necessity to listen. I weel take my port with me as I go. If I do not see you later, Justin, I weel see you tomorrow. We will haff ze long chat, about music, about life—and ozzer things." She stood up and took her glass of ruby wine. The two men stood, and as Sonya passed Lark, the tips of her fingers touched his cheek lightly, as if in promise.

Lark leaned back in his chair, sipping the excellent port, as Verloff quickly got down to cases. "Lark, I know a great deal more about you than you think," he said, stabbing with his cigar. "I wired my representatives in Denver. Once you were a wealthy man, eh? Until the wolves gathered in a pack and took everything away from you?"

"They didn't do it without one hell of a fight," Lark said harshly. He had to admire the meticulous way Allan Pinkerton's people had built up that cover story. No detail had been too small for their attention, if they thought it might be the subject of inquiry. Verloff seemed convinced by it.

"You killed two men, they say. Self-defense, the law agreed, and let you off. But I find it an odd coincidence that the two were the ringleaders of the mining cabal which bankrupted you."

"Plain coincidence, Verloff," Lark said with an enigmatic smile. "Just let it go at that. But I'll say one thing—I'll never be the mark, the victim, again. Since that day, I take, I don't donate. And when I see the chance for the big score, I intend to be just as brutal and merciless as they were, if need be."

"I like your spirit, Lark. Join up with me. With me to plan and you to act, we can hold this entire country in the palms of our hands within five years." The Pole leaned back, smiling at his thoughts, his eyes narrowed against the drift of cigar smoke.

"It would take good men," Lark said.

Verloff spread his hands. "You work with the tools at hand, Lark. Tools that are imperfect, or cracked, or dull of edge. The minds—most are stupid, and greedy. I have had some of my most brilliant plans disrupted because men failed me, or worse, disregarded my instructions. Oh, they paid dearly for that, but punishment didn't put the clink of gold in my pocket."

"If Starbolt is an example . . ."

"Starbolt, ah yes. I'm not displeased that you handled my foreman so roughly, Lark. Perhaps he'll realize now that he is not the king of the dunghill. In sharp, hard action he has proven able enough, but to lead—Lark, Starbolt is not bright, not really bright."

"Tries to go his own way, eh?"

"Yes, and with poor results. The unnecessary killing of the guard Percy was one instance—it stirred up the Robbins and Tucker people beyond all reason."

Lark's heart leaped. Here it was, in a single sentence, the confirmation of his suspicions. The end of the cord at Magma had proven frayed and unusable, but he had felt the bight of it leading past Stoneman's Gap, past Box B and XL, inexorably toward Rail Fence. This was the puzzle piece, the key he had been looking for. Now he could get on with it.

9

Rail Fence Ranch
July 12, 1887

Dear Aunt Susan:
  Having a fine visit here, Miss Verloff is charming, the house beautiful. I have taken employment with Mr. Verloff, to help in some promotions he has under way. He is a very large operator, with many important connections.
  Find I need information on correlation of activity of both European party and Titian-haired group. Dates, amounts, transactions. Do they fit together. Wire Mr. C. to dig out what he can and get it to me through Mr. T.
  My employer has raised the offer for the inn to sixty thousand. Wants it bad. Why? Check on any

activity not yet known which might make it more valuable.

Suggest the bear keep adding to the honey-pot and not move it until its size is too great to pass up.

Rail Fence Land & Cattle Co. is also offering to buy Anchor, bringing commitments to $100,000. Would like XL as well, but Mr. Powell will not sell. Could he lose it by other means?

Will soon send word when it would be best for your family from the east to visit this country. By end of the current month, I hope.

Your aff. nephew,

Justin

P.S. Send me a good small guitar, not too expensive. Charge to my acct.

◄◄◄◄◄◄◄◄◄◄◄◄◄◄◄◄◄◄◄◄◄◄◄◄◄◄◄◄◄◄◄

Lark walked through the front door of Stoneman's Inn, beating the dust from his trousers with his equally dusty hat. Lolly Bailor came toward him, her eyes wide in surprise.

"Why, Mr. Lark!" she exclaimed. "What are you . . . why, I thought . . ."

Lark patted the girl on the shoulder. "Remember, Lolly, I told you things are not always what they seem? They aren't. Tell me, have any of your family been bothering you?"

"Haven't seen a one of 'em except Marsh. Mr. Lark, Marsh wants to get away from the ranch, too. Could you help him?"

"We'll see; maybe later, kid. When you see him again, tell him that if he's careful of the company he keeps, it might be that I could work something out. Is Miss Rimi around?"

"In the kitchen. I'll get her." And the redhead hurried away.

Rimi Woodford came quickly, almost running. She put a hand in Lark's. "Justin, Justin, are you all right?"

"Sure I am," he said. "Don't I look as if I was getting fat and sassy on that good Rail Fence grub?"

She stepped back and gave him a critical survey.

"No, you must be losing it all, sparking the beautiful Sonya.'

He laughed. "She's a lovely dish, all right, though she scares me a little. Those are deep waters, Rimi. Behind that beautiful façade there's a brain as sudden and acute as a steel trap."

"She's a complex person, no doubt of that. But I like her, she's got . . . Justin, does it look right for you to come here? After our bitter quarrel, I mean?"

"The fight served my purpose," he said. "It gave the Rail Fence people a credible reason for my going there, an air of verisimilitude. Now it's time to make up. Rimi, I'll tell you this, your performance in our little farce was *A number One.* For my money, you have Ellen Terry backed right off the boards."

"Thank you, kind sir," she said, dimpling, and dropped him a little curtsy. "I did have an excellent supporting cast."

"Me and old Con?" he laughed. He handed her a letter. "Rimi, make sure this goes by next mail. Brought it myself, don't trust our local delivery service."

She took the envelope. "Aunt Susan again, eh? Justin, there are some men waiting for the stage who are strangers to me, so come in while I sort mail. We can talk without being overheard."

She went behind the post-office counter and laid out some letters. He leaned on elbows at the end where he could watch the doors and the lobby. He asked, "You expect Con pretty soon?"

She looked up at the Seth Thomas. "In less than a half hour. Con's prompt—he's a better driver than you were."

"Oh, I don't know," he objected, laughing. "Didn't I earn my pay? You're beginning to like that Con, eh, Rimi?"

To his surprise she colored a little. "Why, I do. Con's a good man, kind and fine and serious."

"And damned reliable—I know," Lark added. "Rimi, to business. I come today as an emissary of the Rail Fence Land and Cattle Company. I bring a new offer from Verloff for your inn—sixty thousand dollars."

She gave a little gasp. "Sascha's raised it? Justin, it's more nearly what it should be. Just think, with that money I could . . ."

"Take my advice—hold off, little one," Lark said. "The Count may know a thing or two we don't. I intend to check it out. Until then, pretty one, don't sign anything, no matter how harmless the paper looks. Remember, not for me nor Sascha Verloff nor anyone else. You're in the driver's seat, and you can dictate terms. It may be that I—well, I may want you to pretend to sell. If you do you'll demand the offered price in full, and *in cash.*"

She looked at him doubtfully. "Justin, you're using me for bait. But I'll go along, even if you haven't told me the whole story. But I can guess—it's Verloff, isn't it?"

"Let's not speculate too much too soon," Lark said. "But I'll keep you in the know all I can without adding to your danger. If anything happened to you because of us . . ." He shook his head, frowning.

"I'm not afraid, not with you and Con on my side," she said bravely. "Whatever is in my power to help break up this evil threat, I intend to do. Oh, Justin, for months I've gone to bed frightened, and woke up frightened, for myself and my friends and the children. Every hard-faced man who goes through on the stage, every stranger who stops here, draws my nerves tighter than the strings on your guitar. We've got to end this siege of terror, we've got to!"

He patted her on the cheek. "Keep calm, honey. Before the aspens turn to gold, and the tamaracks are flaming candles on the mountainsides, you'll see Starr Valley and Antelope Flats and all the Padlocks sleeping peacefully under the autumn sun, and justice and right will have prevailed!"

"My, but we are poetic!" she said witheringly. "But if that redundancy of words means soon, I'll excuse you. But I can't push away the dread that there will be gunfire and bloodshed before all this is over."

"I hope not, but I can't guarantee it," he said. "Rimi, how have things been going with your inn?"

"Very well, surprisingly. Travel is up, and so is my revenue. It seems that people forget easily, Justin. It

94

has been a few weeks since the last holdup, and it might as well have been ten years ago, for all people seem to worry. Phil's a great help; he has a fine garden coming along, which cuts down on expenses. And the Magma shuttle has been full every day."

"And how is Lolly doing?"

"My redhaired assistant? Justin, the girl is a marvelous help. Of course she's somewhat dreamy after young Cliff Longway has been here, which is as often as he can get out from under Ted Powell's watchful eye."

"Did she say anything about taking on her brother Marsh, who wants to get away from Box B? I met him once, he seems to have possibilities."

"When you leave, when Con leaves . . ." There was doubt in her voice. "I'll need another man, but I'm not sure I want another Bailor around the place. What do you think, Justin?"

"You might be saving him from that moral pigsty."

"All right, I'll tell Lolly to pass the word for him to come and see me."

"Good girl. But Rimi, talk to him like a Dutch uncle before you put him to work. Let him know if his foot slips just once, he's done. Of course Lolly will see to it . . . Say, here comes your Magma stage. I'll give Con a hand."

When stage passengers and baggage had been unloaded, and the vehicle and teams turned over to Phil, Lark and Con Tetrault went back into the inn. "Con, we've got to powwow," Lark said.

"While I sort the mail, why don't you two palaver down at the end of the room?" Rimi asked. "I'll keep an eye on any intruders."

"Thanks, kid," Lark said. When they were comfortable on a settee, he asked, "Anything new, Con?"

"I'm getting the feel of things," Tetrault said. "And I'm in solid with Art Rankine. A couple of days ago I pointed out to him a green-goods man who was wanted in five states. Art nabbed the crook, and will pick up a nice reward."

"Which he is welcome to, since Pinkerton's never accept rewards," Lark said.

"Yeah, when he offered to split with me, I had a

95

hard time backing out of it. So I'm aces with Art, though I don't like that night marshal of his."

"Flaherty? He has the look of a heavy drinker."

"Right, and the nose, too. He's a gambler, Justin, always broke. And I've seen him talking to Pike Sumter—he's a Bailor shirttail."

"Keep an eye on him, Con, though I doubt if Flaherty is fooling Rankine very much. We might find a use for Flaherty, so don't cross him. You saw the Bear Consolidated man?"

"Anderson, the super? Yep, though I didn't spill much. Told him I represented his head office in Mantoul, and was working under cover. He said he appreciated being told, and he confirmed orders that he was to allow the gold cleanup to keep building, until he got orders to ship. It worried him a little. He's a good man, I think, and honest. And he hates the Redtops."

"Then we'll let him in on the play when the time comes. What about Ben Parchman?"

Tetrault rubbed his chin. "I don't know just what to make of Old Sourpuss. Not married, doesn't gamble, lives frugally by himself. No indications that he's on the crook. He's not an easy man to get next to."

"We won't cross him off yet," Lark said. "Con, you done a fine job. But you'll have to keep at it."

"I know. We'll get together when you're ready to move?"

"Yes. But Con, we can't move on suspicion. And with the state of law enforcement which seems to prevail, in my opinion our best bet, if not our only bet, is to catch the crooks in the act. That means big bait and big risks, and likely more than a little powder burned."

"You don't trust Pete Looby, the sheriff?"

"Write him off," Lark said emphatically. "He's as deep in Verloff's pocket as a man can get. And his deputies with him. There are U.S. marshals at Fort Ruskin and Coryell; we might try to bring them in for the finale. Trouble is, both marshals are overworked, and about the time we need them, they'll be off to hellangone tracking renegades or hunting horse thieves."

"Looks as if we'd better count on our own army," Tetrault said. "You have some glimmers about how to rig the scheme?"

"I've got it roughed out. Aunt Susan will send in the rest of the boys, and sometime in the next ten days we'll get together for a confab. We'll tie it all together—the bait, the trap, and the hungry rats. It has to be a single-shot deal, Con; if we don't grab the whole kit and caboodle in one fell swoop, this country is so damn big we'll lose some of 'em. I want to tie up every single loose end."

"I've seen you work before, Justin. I'll bet you've already got something cooking that will make our Aunt Susan chuckle in her rocking chair, as she knits a rope for the hangman."

Lark laughed. "I wish it were that easy. Anything else, Con?"

"Yeah, one thing—I ran into a drummer in Magma; he's on the road with ladies' and gents' clothing and such. He went through that same holdup you did, the Redtops. Over a beer he tells me that one thing struck him funny, being in his line—the robber with the gloves on. The drummer says it's his guess that man's middle finger is gone; the way it moved, the glove finger was stuffed with cloth or cotton."

"I think he's right. That would be Lippy Bailor, then, right now one of Verloff's hired hands. I'll bet he was there before that holdup as well as after. Con, we're getting closer."

"Close enough to get burned," Tetrault said dryly. "When will we get together again?"

"Now that Rimi and I have publicly buried the hatchet, I'll set up a meet through her. One thing—I'm expecting a letter from Collins that might be real dynamite. If it reached Verloff it would be Katy-bar-the-door. When it comes to you, figure a way to get it to me secretly, but pronto."

"I'll think of something, even if it takes more play-acting," Tetrault said with a grin. "Y'know, Justin, I thought Rimi and I showed real talent the other day. Maybe the theater could use us."

"Oh, undoubtedly. You could play Romeo, with Rimi standing on the upper balcony in the light of

97

the moon, while you spouted the Bard's romantic stanzas. A pair to draw to, I'd say."

"Well, I hope it wouldn't be *Love's Labour's Lost,*" Tetrault said. "I like that girl, Justin." He glanced over at Rimi, her fair head bowed over her ledger.

"Don't blame you," Lark said. "Unfortunately, this isn't any time to mix business with pleasure."

"No? What about you and the lovely Sonya?"

Lark laughed, and struck Tetrault hard on the shoulder muscle with his fist. "That could very well be business too, old top," he said.

He left Tetrault to his thoughts and plans. At the desk he paused to say goodbye to Rimi. Frowning, she said, "Justin, I hope you and Con will be careful. You're tough, but your hide won't stop a forty-five slug."

"We'll be good," he promised. "Now you be careful of strangers, and don't take any wooden nickels. We worry about you, pretty one."

He rode west on Mingus, the gray mule, deep in thought. Lark had refused Verloff's offer of any of the fine mounts in the Rail Fence string. The mule, cross-grained, cranky, and independent, just fitted Lark's mood. Two of a kind, maybe, he thought. And the Rail Fence horse might be a stolen one, for all I know.

Rail Fence had not only a large horse herd, but it seemed to Lark an unusually large bunch of men on its payroll, more than even a large spread required. Some good cowhands, but he thought a disproportionate number of drifters, hard-eyed, competent, short of temper. Men of Rod Starbolt's type. Lark had not had any direct trouble with Starbolt, who was still walking twisted from his encounter with Lark. Lark resolved to give the man no chance ever to get behind him, for that could well be fatal. Verloff, moreover, had eased Starbolt out of much of his former authority, and the man didn't like it.

Verloff was sitting at an ornate desk in his small office off the parlor. Lark reported Rimi's continued refusal of the rancher's offer. "But I have talked her into being friends again," he reported. "And I think I'm getting her softened up to selling the place. Another visit or two, and she'll be ready to sign. One sticker, though; she's insisting on cash."

Verloff rose, and walked to the window. He stood looking out for a minute, his hands clasped behind his back, his fingers working, his only sign of nervousness. He came back to the desk.

"My offer is more than the place is worth, nor will I hold it open forever," he said, frowning. "As for cash —well, I suppose that can be managed. Push her, Lark, push her! I need that place, need it badly. There's a deadline . . ." He brought the edge of his fist down on the desk so the inkwell jumped. "Lark, I told you Fredericks will sell, but he too wants cash. Which puts me damned near over the barrel in that regard. A temporary thing, Lark, you understand, temporary. But I've never been one to shilly-shally; I'll work this out. This opportunity may never come again. I don't dare to miss it."

" 'There is a tide in the affairs of men, which, taken at the flood, leads on to fortune,' " Lark quoted.

" 'Omitted, all the voyage of their life is bound in shallows and in miseries,' " Verloff capped it. "Which describes very well my situation at the moment, Lark." He sounded a bit worried. He pushed back his swivel chair and began pacing once again, back and forth across the small room. He struck a fist into the open palm of his other hand. "If only word would come from Magma . . ." Lark heard him mutter.

"Magma?" Lark asked casually.

Verloff's head came up. "Uh, yes—a mining deal there. Some property I am gambling on, where we expect to strike a valuable lode almost any time. I'm waiting for word on it; just one of my minor ventures. You see, Lark, we entrepreneurs diversify our holdings, so the risks are averaged. And some of my projects are damned risky at the moment, I can tell you," he said.

Lark nodded, without voicing the thought that ran like the glow of a spark through his mind—you don't know the half of it, Sascha Verloff.

10

Dear Aunt Susan:

I hope your visiting relatives will arrive here by the 22nd inst. so I will be here to meet them and show them the points of interest about Stoneman's Gap.

Mr. Verloff is waiting for word on a business venture in Magma, and then plans to go bear hunting. He has given me more responsibility since Rod Starbolt, his former foreman, met a sudden and tragic fate recently.

If I can get away, a Mr. Anderson, who is in the mining business in Magma, wants me to ride to Mantoul with one of their special rigs. I told him I would like to go but would be tied up until July 24th. He said he thought the rig would not leave until that date, but he would give me positive word when he had it. In that case I might reach Denver a few days thereafter, if his Mantoul office puts their OK as to the date of the 24th.

If you can reach Uncle Allan, mention that the Chicago office of the Great Pacific Railway might have data on this part of the country. It is rumored that they have maps of an earlier survey, but cannot confirm here.

Take care of yourself and write soon.

Your aff. nephew,
Justin

<<<<<<<<<<<<<<<<<<<<<<<<<<<<<<<<

Sonya met Lark at the foot of the stair. She said, with a purr of her voice, "Justin, you haff been neglecting me. Not one time yet haff you been riding with me. I would like much to show you zis country. And zis morning I am so bored with all zis—zis business affairs of my brother's."

"Well, your brother's my boss, and he keeps me busy," Lark said. He stared at her in frank admiration. She looked lovely in a green riding habit, long of skirt, the tight bodice showing to advantage her graceful bosom and her slim waist. The boyish hat with its long pheasant plume gave her face a piquant air.

"But I haff asked, and today he has given you a reprieve," she said. "You haff not ze excuse of duty. So we go riding."

"Certainly I won't object. But do you speak for your brother?"

"In all things important," she said, dimpling. "Sascha is w'at you call ze man of action. But me, I am ze deep thinker. I sit back and watch ze worl' move, and make plans, very intricate, very expansive."

"And you give them to Sascha to follow?" he asked.

Her laugh was musical, self-deprecating. "Not often does he pay attention to them, which annoys me. I see those beautiful webs which I weave go pouf!—like ze snow in ze spring sun." Taking his arm, she turned him toward the front door of the mansion. "So you mus' follow this time my plan—we will ride over the green meadows which now turn brown, down ze swift creeks which turn into rills, and we ride up ze hills, from where we can see ze countryside, all ze way to ze edge of ze great sky. Justin, I weel show you all ze kingdoms of ze worl'!"

Amused, Lark thought: thus did Satan, also. But that was man to man, or demon to God. This woman is lovely, so even her temptations are a pleasure. Though I have things to do that must be done, they will have to stand in abeyance for the day, for she seems in a mood to talk. And if she talks—well, I can't believe she is completely in the dark about her brother's plans.

"Give me a few minutes," he said, and hurried up to his room. There he removed the hideout derringer and its holster, and in its stead strapped on openly a cartridge belt with an S. & W. Schofield .45 in the holster. I might need more firepower and faster than the little gun offers, he thought. Nor will it look out of place, for all these Rail Fence hands pack six-guns. "Snake country," one of them had explained to Lark, though he hadn't seen any snake more inimical than a garter snake.

They rode down the lane to the main gate and turned north. Sonya, sidesaddle on a sleek roan mare, handled her horse with the negligent ease of the expert rider. Lark, feeling that Mingus the mule was too bourgeois for such elegant company, had chosen a rangy black gelding from the ranch string. The horses were frisky under the slant of the morning sun, and Sonya urged her mare at a good pace along the Fort Ruskin Road.

Southwest of them, the crisp ridge of the Coyote Hills swept all the way to the Padlocks, separating Padlock Valley from the Antelope Flats. The rolling slopes rose to a respectable elevation. In the East they would be high enough and jagged enough to be called mountains, but here they were mere hills. Sonya turned her mare west from the road onto a trail that climbed out of the valley up into rock ledges and scattered scrub pines.

The horses were panting a bit and their hides were sheened with sweat when Sonya halted her mare on a point that looked out over the valley, above a sheer drop.

"Here," she said. "Justin, please to help me down."

He dismounted and tied the gelding. Sonya disengaged her knee from the horn of the sidesaddle, and as he reached up, she slid from the saddle into his arms. Both arms around her, he held her, and she did not move to disengage herself from him. She turned her face up, her dark eyes enormous and liquid, her lips slightly parted over pearly teeth. Now her eyes went shut, the long lashes quivering.

Lark pulled her against him, and his mouth found hers. The kiss was long and demanding, her lips responding hotly, avidly seeking.

When she broke away, her breath was coming quickly. She held him at arm's length, staring up at him, the shadow of a smile on her lips and in her eyes. He took her hands, more than a little shaken at the sudden passion of this beautiful woman. At last he released her.

"All the cities of the world?" he asked softly.

She laughed, and taking his arm, led him to the brink of the drop. In a possessive gesture, her arm flung out toward the green of the valley bottom, the massive peaks of the Running Wolfs beyond, and the notch, dimly discernible in the distance, of Stoneman's Gap, where the silver snake of the Redstone River dove into its slash of rock and was gone.

"Justin, you mus' look—ze reach of it, ze height, ze depth! Once I was of ze city, Justin, ze small close houses, ze many people, ze air a tight envelope filled with ze smells of men and animals, ze horizon low and gray and jus' beyond ze fingertips. But zis—in zis country, I expand, I spread, I am inflated like ze toy balloon. I am filled with wonder, even now I cannot believe zis country. I could not go back, not ever, I want all of eet—for my life as long as I live, for my grave when I come to die. You understand this, no?"

He tightened his arm about her shoulders. "Of course I understand," he said, feeling a rapport with this woman even deeper than the accord he felt with Rimi Woodford. She has the enthusiasm of the convert, he thought, one who has known the cities and found them wanting. "How can anyone look out on that scene without feeling the grandeur of it? It makes one feel small. I'm not a religious man, but . . ."

"Here you feel God is not far away, eh?" she asked, smiling. "Justin, would you like to stay here, to live, to be ze king of your own domain? With my help, to build this land into the finest ranch in all ze Territory?"

Surprised, Lark looked at her speculatively. "Ah, those far-flung plans of yours, eh? You are trying to tempt me, my dear? What of Sascha?"

She shook her head. "Ze man of action? Justin, my brother is a man of unusual gifts, but he does not think deeply. He moves on impulse, and I am afraid zat some day he will overreach himself. Then zat 'ouse of cards he has built will come tumbling down." There was a hint of sadness in her voice.

He probed carefully, as delicately as a surgeon lancing an infected carbuncle. "Sascha has some dangerous ideas, then?"

She did not answer for a space, looking north up the Fort Ruskin road as it wound like a gray ribbon along the near side of the Redstone. Turning to Lark then, she said, "Justin, my brother is torn by ze ambition which feeds on him like ze vulture. He was a very young man when our family, which was of ze *petit noblesse,* lost everything—fortune, jewels, land, everything. Sascha came to America, he vows he weel become important man, bigger, more powerful, than ze powerful men who have driven our family to poverty in Poland." She spread her hands. "He work hard, he go to school nights. In Chicago, he start to make ze business deals, ver' successful. He marries a woman of some wealth. When she die five, maybe six years ago, she leaves him her wealth; not a great fortune, but ze very fine sum. Then he send for me to come from Poland."

"You were the only one of your family left?" he asked.

"Yes, jus' Sascha and me. Oh, we have cousins, great-uncles, other relations, but none close. I am studying violin, piano, on—w'at you call, scholarship —and when I come to Chicago, I expect to live there, learn ze English, perhaps master ze violin to play on ze concert stage. But only six months am I there. Then Sascha moves to Montana and I mus' come along. After he buy Rail Fence, he tell me, 'Sonya, beyond zis log house, you weel build us a new house, finest in all ze valley. You design, you supervise, you choose furnishings. You must see that I have house twice so goot as Count Karolyi's house in Poland, you remember? Spend whatever you must, my sister. Or do you want me to send you back to Poznan?' " She laughed, a bit ruefully. "Of course I do not want to go back. So for three years I spend all my time building our so beautiful house. Jus' last year, she is almost finish', and we move in. Now is nobody come to see us. So Sascha, he plan to be still bigger man, invite all great men here, maybe governor, or senator, on even terms. Maybe he go in politics himself."

Lark said carefully, "For all this—well, his inher-

104

itance from his late wife must have been a large one."

She shook her head. "What come from his wife, all that go to buy ze original Rail Fence. For ozzer deals, he invests money for rich people back in Poland, he buys and sells, I do not know many things he do. Sometimes I think he—w'at you say, stick hees neck out?—so I am glad you are to work with him now, Justin. You have ze head mos' level. Maybe you can keep him from being too impetuous, too rash—too ruthless."

"I'm afraid your brother is not a man to accept advice from others, Sonya," Lark said. "What does he do that frightens you?"

"No, no, I cannot talk about eet. That ees for Sascha to tell you, when he ees ready, and if he has decided to use you for his plans, as he has me." She was silent then, staring across the valley. The edge of bitterness in her last words surprised him.

Damn the woman! he thought. She's lovely and tantalizing, and a far cry from stupid. So is she revealing these differences between her and her brother for her own reasons? Is she weaving a devious web to trap a buzzing fly named Justin Lark? Was the passion in those sweet lips real, or pure calculation? Go slow, Justin, go slow, he told himself. Don't let your sympathy for this lonely girl blind you to the dangers.

Sonya broke the tenor of his thoughts. "Look, Justin," she cried, pointing a finger toward the scene below them. "There is ze stage from Fort Ruskin. How delightful—eet look like a toy coach, pulled by six mice, like in ze fairy tale."

"From the roil of dust, Mulcahy is cracking his whip," Lark said. He snapped open the hunting case of his watch. "And no wonder, he's running twenty minutes late."

"So clear is ze air, one can almost make out ze buckles on ze harness," Sonya said, leaning forward over the precipitous drop. Then her hand tightened on Lark's arm. "Look, Justin! Two men, zey have come from those bushes. Now zey ride out in front of ze coach."

"And the stage is stopping!" Lark exclaimed. "They're down from their horses, and there's the passengers, getting out and lining up beside the coach."

"Ees a holdup!" Sonya said excitedly. "Oh, no, not anozzer! I thought maybe—Justin, should we ride ver' fast down to ze road to help them?"

Lark, frowning grimly, shook his head. "Not a chance to get there in time. Let's watch to see if we can tell where the bandits go afterwards. Sonya, look at those two bandits!"

"I have ver' good eyes, but . . . yes, yes, I see now, zey have something red over their faces."

"The knitted red masks the Redtops wear," he said. "Or someone copying them. Damn, they've got a nerve! A stage holdup right out in the open, not even waiting for Dead Man's Canyon."

Intently, he and Sonya watched the unfolding of the drama far below. It was like the tiny stage of a puppet show. One man stood back, while the other mingled with the four passengers. Then the men ran to their waiting horses. As they mounted, one of the tiny figures beside the stagecoach ran forward. There was the bloom of powder smoke, and the man fell to the ground. Seconds later Lark heard the distant shot, like the snapping of a twig.

"My God, I hope that wasn't Mulcahy!" Lark exclaimed. "Look, Sonya, the robbers have disappeared into the brush to the east, toward your ranch. Let's get down to that coach."

Sonya, riding like a Cossack, led the way down the steep hill at a breakneck pace. They reached the intersection with the road and raced north. Only a quarter of a mile further, and the Concord came hurtling toward them around a bend, the dust spinning in a high plume behind it. Lark, halting his horse plainly in the open, raised an open palm high. The driver reined in his six-horse hitch and stomped on the brake pedal. In a shrill screech of brakeblocks and a drifting cloud of dust, the heavy vehicle shuddered to a stop.

"Mulcahy, thank God you're all right!" Lark said, riding up close. "We saw the whole thing from up on the hill. Who got hurt, and how bad?"

"One of my passengers. He got mad and cussed out the two robbers as they started to ride away, and they shot him. Got him in the leg, not too bad. He'll make it to the inn all right, and Miss Rimi will patch him

106

up. Damn it all, Lark, why do they keep pickin' on me?" Mulcahy showed his disgust by spitting a great splash of tobacco juice into the dust of the road.

"Might be your plain bad luck, and it might not," Lark said. "What did the robbers get?"

"Not a hell of a lot, mebbe six hundred from the passengers, and nothin' a-tall from the strongbox or the mail, we wasn't carrying a thing of value. My man that got shot, he was packin' about four hundred in dust, the dam' fool. That's why he was mad."

"Can't blame him too much. You'd better move along, Mulcahy. You want us to get word about it to Fort Ruskin?"

"Hell, no. I'll make a report in Mantoul. Won't do no good in Fort Ruskin; you mention 'Redtops' to Pete Looby, and the sheriff and his deppities crawl under the desk like prairie dogs poppin' into holes. Oh say, Lark, I got somethin' for you."

Mulcahy fumbled under the worn thin pad on the seat, and brought out a large flat envelope. "Feller in Fort Ruskin ast me to drop it off at the inn for you. Said it was a pitcher he didn't want cracked or tore, so he couldn't mail it. So as long as you're right here, I'll give it to you."

Taking the envelope, Lark said, "Thanks, Mulcahy. I know what it is, a picture of my Aunt Susan. A dear old lady, my only relative. She said she was sending the picture by some traveler."

"Lucky the Redtops didn't get it; they've took damn near everything else in the country," Mulcahy grumbled. Lark grinned and reined his horse aside as the driver released the brake and cracked his long whip over the ears of the leaders. The Concord swept away, the slow dust drifting toward the hill. Lark joined Sonya, and as soon as the light breeze had dissipated the hanging dust, they rode fast toward the Rail Fence lane.

"Your brother won't be pleased at a holdup right on your doorstep," Lark said.

"He weel be ver' angry," Sonya agreed. "Sascha like for ze law to be strict when he want it to be, and if he think it do not fit his way, then eet should be

107

changed." She gave him a glance that he found as enigmatic as her last statement.

They rode into the ranch yard just as Sascha Verloff came down the steps of the ranchhouse. The rancher hadn't been home much of late, and he had not confided in Lark or Sonya exactly what business was taking him away. Lark did know Verloff had been as far as Mantoul. When he had returned the evening before, the rancher had not been in a particularly pleasant mood.

Sonya started talking even before her brother could help her down from her horse. Her words tumbled over each other as she recited the tale of the holdup.

"And they shot a man, Sascha, not bad, ze driver say. Eet was like ze balcony of a theater, where we were, so clearly could we see ze play enacted. Two ver' bold men, with red hoods over their heads. Ze loot was maybe six hundred of dollars."

Lark, standing quiet, holding the reins of his horse, saw angry blood rise in Verloff's face. A vein in the man's temple swelled and throbbed, his lips tightened to a thin line. Lark heard him say softly, as if to himself, "That's what they just rode in from, as bold as brass! The idiots, the Goddamned idiots! After all I've done . . ." Then he turned to Lark and said, "Lark, you wait right here. I'll be back in a minute."

He went up the veranda steps two at a time, but at the top he stopped. He shouted toward the barn, "Damn you, Howdy, you get over here and take care of these horses!" Without waiting for an answer, he jerked open the door and rushed into the house.

Howdy, the hostler, came scuttling from the barn. Avoiding Sonya's glance, he grabbed the reins of the horses and hurried away. Lark looked a question at Sonya, but she shook her head; she did not want to go into the house. They waited.

Verloff came striding out, wearing a jacket now. He looked neither right nor left, but walked purposefully past the end of the bunkhouse toward the long log ranchhouse which had served Rail Fence until the fine new house was built. Now part of the old house had been made into rooms for the half-dozen servants. One end of it, perhaps a third, had been re-modeled into quarters for the ranch foreman.

Verloff stopped a dozen feet from the foreman's door and stood rigid, his feet, slightly apart, planted solidly. Lark saw the man take a deep breath, and brace himself. Unobtrusively, Lark touched Sonya's arm, and drew her well aside.

Sascha Verloff called loudly, "All right, Starbolt, come out here! This instant!"

The seconds dragged, and time stretched intermi-nably. Then the door opened, and the foreman came out on the porch. He stood there above Verloff, in-solently, his thumbs hooked in the leather of the gun-belt around his lean middle. He said, "Yeah. What you want, Verloff?"

"You call me 'Mr. Verloff,' Starbolt," the rancher said coldly. "You've gone against my orders. You've tried to think for yourself, and it's gone badly. I want to know why."

Lark saw the foreman's eyes flick toward him, then away, as if dismissing Lark as negligible. Lark saw an-other man come quietly around the corner of the log house and stand motionless, watching the scene, tautly tense. Lippy Bailor.

"Answer me, you punk!" Verloff snapped. He was leaning forward angrily, hands jammed deep in his jacket pockets.

"I ain't been treated right, *Mister* Verloff," the fore-man said. "I was your *segundo* for a long time, until this ranny come along. Then you forgot I run every job for you without one single hitch. You kick me aside, put Lark in ahead of me, move him up to the big house even. Me'n the boys ain't gonna stand for that, Verloff. We figger it's time we looked out for our own interests. After all, we know plenty about what goes on, and we figger we oughtta be partners, not just hired hands. So just for a sample, we took the stage this morning, without any of your fancy planning. Worked out right well, too."

"Why, you fools, don't you realize what you're do-ing?" Verloff asked. "You're jeopardizing everything we've all worked for, all I've planned for a span of

109

years—just for a handful of chicken feed—chicken feed, Starbolt!"

"Chicken feed, maybe, but you ain't gettin' the big split of it this time, mister. The time when we was afraid of you is past, Verloff. You ain't about to ditch us. We know too much. From now on . . ."

"You think you can blackmail Sascha Verloff?" the rancher demanded, his voice strident. "You can swear all you want about any orders I gave you, and all you'll do is swear a noose around your own neck. Nobody, Starbolt, nobody in this whole country would believe your word against mine. I'm a big man around here, Starbolt, and don't you forget it."

The foreman gave him a feral grin. "That *big* is all in your own head, Verloff. And now it's about to get cut down to size. I've decided this operation will run much better without you. Then it will belong to the girl, and I can handle her. With me giving the orders, we'll see some real action around here."

Verloff laughed mirthlessly. "You haven't the brains to run a sheep-shearing. Starbolt, you're through—"

"Shut up! You've said your piece!" Starbolt said, and his hand swept toward his gun.

The gun was just halfway out of the holster when there came the sound of a shot, oddly muffled from Verloff's side. Starbolt toppled forward, his eyes wide with shock and surprise. He tumbled down the steps, his revolver clattering to the boards. Verloff took a step forward, and Lark fired past him, two quick shots. Lippy Bailor crumpled, his six-gun firing harmlessly once into the porch roof as he fell.

Gun in hand, Lark ran to the end of the building, but there was no one else in sight. He swung toward the bunkhouse, but it was quiet, its door empty. He nudged the limp body of Lippy Bailor with a boot toe, and sure that the man was dead, he holstered his pistol.

Sonya was standing motionless, her hands to her face, her eyes wide with shock. Verloff stripped off his jacket and was beating at the blackened cloth smoldering at the pocket. The jacket sagged with the weight of the little gun Verloff had carried concealed in the pocket. He had fired through the cloth.

Looking at the rancher, Lark thought he could see the slightest of smiles, as if things had gone well. He had the feeling that the act had played according to Verloff's script—the rancher had said his lines, Starbolt had reacted correctly, Verloff had held out the bait and Starbolt had grabbed at it, and died thereby. Lippy Bailor had been the only unforeseen quantity, but Verloff's confidence in Lark had not been misplaced, and Lark had killed Bailor for him. Now there would be no more interference with Verloff's plans, no possible talking out of turn. The man had even managed to give his sister a lesson in the dangers of crossing his will.

Lark's gorge rose, and he swallowed quickly, fighting nausea. He had killed men before, but that had been because he had to. But here he had been forced to act as an unpaid executioner, his victim set up in advance. Lark found it sickening, disgusting. Only a great effort kept him from telling Verloff so.

Now a woman came from the house, the woman who called herself Mrs. Starbolt. She stood at the top of the steps, staring down at the foreman's body. Her round, featureless face was blank. Her soft, too-fat body was misshapen by the child that was beginning in her belly. She came heavily down the steps. Reaching down, she pulled from under Starbolt's vest a red object, and Verloff took it from her. It was a hood knitted of red yarn, with an opening for the eyes, the type of headgear that Lark had heard his mother call a "balaklava."

"Look here, Lark," Verloff said, holding it up. "Starbolt intended to use the reputation of the Redtops. They'll be blamed for the stage holdup these two pulled this morning."

"It looks that way," Lark said noncommittally. "A good thing you were ready for him, Sascha,"

"He's had dreams of grandeur for quite a while, big ideas of what he would do, the fool. And he was jealous of you, Lark."

The woman spoke for the first time, her voice dull. "You didn't have to go for to kill him, Mr. Verloff. He always did your bidding until you brung in somebody else over his head. That hurt him, Mr. Verloff."

111

"I don't need your opinions, Amy," Verloff snapped. "Nor your advice. Did he keep you informed of all he did?"

She shook her head, the movement as measured as a metronome. "Now and again, but only like, we would be rich some day, and our kids . . . we was gonna get married . . ."

"And his stupidity ended all that, when he drew down on me," Verloff said brusquely. "You're from Magma, Amy? Plan to get your things packed and leave for there in the next couple of days. I'll pay your stage fare. But he must have left you some money. You take that and the rest of his belongings. And I'll give you his last pay and a bit extra. But Amy, no talking, you hear? About the Redtops, or Rail Fence, or Sascha Verloff—if I hear that you are, I warn you it will go hard with you."

She nodded slowly. "I know better'n to talk, Mr. Verloff. All I can think of right now is to see Rod is buried decent. You'll see to that?"

Verloff patted her on the shoulder. "I'll have Howdy and Jules and Pendergast dig the graves up on the hillside. We'll have the funeral this afternoon."

"One thing more—a cross on the grave, please, Mr. Verloff." Her voice held only darkness.

"And a cross," Verloff promised.

The double funeral that afternoon was short, and perfunctory except for Verloff, in as crass an exhibition of hypocrisy as Lark had ever observed, reading the Twenty-Third and the Thirty-Ninth psalms. He read them with a certain unctuous solemnity that seemed to go down well with the assembled hands, and, Lark thought, maybe sincerely enough according to the man's lights.

As Howdy and Jules and Pendergast shoveled dirt back into the twin graves (for such menial work was scorned by horsemen like the cowhands), Sonya Verloff walked a little higher up the hill. Then, clear and sweet over the curving arc of the valley came the sobbing notes of her violin, soaring in a threnody that was, Lark thought, probably more than the two men deserved. It is kind of Sonya, more kindly than any act of mine. For the first time, the woman Amy

112

is showing emotion, the tears at last flowing down her forlorn, pale face.

And when it was over, it was Sonya who put her arm around the woman and led her, still weeping, down the hillside path toward the ranch buildings.

11

Rail Fence Ranch
July 22, 1887

Dear Aunt Susan:

Your relatives have arrived and I have sent them sightseeing. Your cousin Val has gone to visit his friend, Mr. Anderson, of Bear Consolidated, in Magma.

I will soon leave from Magma to help escort a special shipment by the mining company to Mantoul. Since I am thus engaged, Mr. Verloff will handle the direction of his newest business venture himself, and I feel it can all be brought to a successful conclusion.

Pieces are now dropping into place like a Chinese puzzle. Our friends will be very helpful in solving it, but I could wish we could count on more aid from Uncle Samuel.

When I reach Mantoul I will wire you.

Your aff. nephew,
Justin

◄◄◄◄◄◄◄◄◄◄◄◄◄◄◄◄◄◄◄◄◄◄◄◄◄◄◄◄◄

Lark walked into the handsome blue bedroom he had been assigned in the big house and shut the door behind him. He unbuckled the heavy gunbelt and dropped it on the bed, heedless of the clean comforter. He sagged into the Morris chair and leaned back, his arms folded, his eyes closed. He felt beat

113

physically and emotionally. He knew from other days that his malaise was a passing thing, for the stimulus of the danger that was sweeping closer with the hours would bring back sharpness to his wits and vigor to his muscles. But at this moment he was tired with the bitter exhaustion of a race badly run. He had been an unwilling player in a cynical drama of betrayal and death.

Any illusions he may have had about his association with Sascha Verloff had been blown away by that shot from the hideout gun that killed Rod Starbolt. Lark, too, would serve Verloff's purpose, and then he would be cast aside, or thrown to the wolves, or left dead in a dry gulch beyond the Fort Ruskin road. Lark did not cavil at that; it was not a new hazard in his perilous trade. He had met other men as ruthless as Sascha Verloff, and faced their challenge, and beaten them. But he had not liked it, and he did not like it now. Always he had the regret, even sorrow, that such men would use their fine intelligence and their gift of leadership in such bootless causes. Was it a mania, Lark wondered, that drove men to ride rough-shod over all opposition? And when that bastion had been crushed, to try for new goals even more merci-less and brutal?

Verloff's piece was locked now into the puzzle Lark was solving. Not so Sonya Verloff—where did she fit? A superb woman, brilliant, vibrant with life, full of promise overt and concealed. Her attraction for Lark was a force both physical and mental, magnetic, almost psychic. He shook his head—why is my rapport with this unusual woman more solid than for the warm friendliness of Rimi Woodford? There is in Sonya the promise of heaven, or the deadly threat of poison. If she is enmeshed in the plans of her brother, she's poi-son. And how could she be ignorant of the empire he was building, when the two were so close?

"Damn!" he swore softly. The problem was intoler-able. He stood up and went to the dresser, where stood the large mounted photograph of his Aunt Susan. He had taken it from the envelope Mulcahy had given him, and placed it in plain sight. He faced it to the light, staring at the sweet-faced old lady in the steel-rimmed glasses, her hair a swirl of white, the lace ruching pristine at the collar of her black dress.

"You old bitch!" he whispered. "You've killed more men, and gotten more good men killed, than any odd old biddy in all America. There are men behind bars in Yuma and Canon City and Deer Lodge who would like to cut you into tiny pieces and feed you to the coyotes. But they don't know you are only a name and a photograph. I'm not so sure some of your own cousins and nephews and nieces wouldn't like to be shut of you too, you old termagant!"

He took a penknife from his pocket. He worked the blade carefully into the thick cardboard of the mount. It resisted at first, then split open. From between the two layers he took a sheet of onionskin paper, covered with fine script. Excitedly, he smoothed it flat and studied its message. Then he found a clean sheet of paper and began tabulating as he read the cryptic listing of information:

5/8/82	Rail Fence Ranch, deed Ott to Verloff	$ 45,000
8/7/83	Redtop—R & T Stage, DMC	13,000
9/15/83	Swinging S Ranch— deed, Lowry to Verloff	28,000
10/12/83	Redtop—Brant-Lochray payroll	16,000
6/12/84	Redtop (?)—Bear Consol. Cleanup	36,000
4/24/85	Bar Cross Ranch— deed, Stone to Verloff	41,000
8/10/85	Fort Ruskin Merc. Co. deed and lien to Rail Fence Land & Cattle Co. total (J.L.—this paid $85,-000 cash, $75,000 note to Ft. Ruskin Terr. Bank., see entry below.)	160,000

9/22/85	Redtop—Magma Bank & Trust holdup	100,000+
12/1/85	Verloff—paid Ft. Ruskin Terr. Bank	75,000
4/13/86	Deed, Coryell Grand Ranche to Rail Fence L. & C. Co. cash	80,000
7/1/86	Redtop—Antelope Flat, Brant-Lochray etc.	8,000
8/12/86	Redtop—Bear Consol. & stage pass. DMC	10,000
8/31/86	Redtop—Mantoul Stage DMC—Bank notes	40,000
9/15/86	Redtop—Coryell express office	23,000
4/12/87	Redtop (?)—Tom Towe shot & killed	0
6/26/87	Redtop—Mantoul-Ft. Ruskin stage DMC	9,500+

J. L.—Some of these
amounts are approxi-
mate but I think
pretty close to the
truth. Your hunch
looks good except
a spot or two.

T.J.C.

Lark completed his tabulation and stared at it. Bless that Ted Collins! he thought. It must have been hell to dig out most of this, but he did it. Here are the building blocks of the Rail Fence Land & Cattle Company. Its growth in a short five years from one medium-sized ranch, Rail Fence, into a sizable empire is phenomenal, to say the least, but even more interesting is the parallel list of robberies and holdups. And there may have been depredations in other areas not included on Ted's list. Lark could not withhold a grudging admiration for Verloff's acuity—the Rail Fence itself grown fourfold, with a grand mansion for headquarters; the Fort Ruskin Merc., a power in the mercantile and freighting business clear to the Canadian border, the Coryell Grand Ranche in the Starr Valley, and soon to be added, by Verloff's own account, Stoneman's Gap and its Inn, the Anchor Ranch, and in the farther future, Powell's XL Ranch. Powell did not want to sell, Lark knew, but that would not deter Verloff. There were ways and means.

The correlation of expenditures and robberies was too close to be a coincidence. The Verloff empire had grown in direct ratio to the exploits of the Redtops, with a few exceptions. The man has a preference for cash transactions almost amounting to mania, Lark thought. Only once had he borrowed, and even that note was paid off within four months. The first half of the payment for the Ft. Ruskin Merc. was the puzzling thing. Lark could find no offsetting robbery or raid to cover it. That fact annoyed Lark, for it confused an otherwise sharp-etched picture.

He slid Collins' sheet back into the photograph mount, pinched the cardboard closed, and wiped away any signs of its removal. He left the picture propped conspicuously on the dresser. As he scratched a match and reduced his own scribbled papers to ash, he thought sardonically, Edgar Allan Poe would have been proud of me. I hope Allan Pinkerton feels the same way.

He leaned back again in the Morris chair, planning. The flow of all things toward a climax was becoming nearly machinelike. Today's murder by Verloff—for murder it was, even though Lark could feel little sympathy for Starbolt or Bailor—improved the chance of success of the final cleanup. Verloff might have assigned direction of the raid to Starbolt, and himself waited in the wings. But now Verloff would have to ramrod the operation, for Lark was too new to be fully trusted, nor did Verloff have what he would consider an adequate hold over him. And Lark intended to extend a bait so fat, so tempting, that Verloff would not think of delegating its collection to any lieutenant.

He wondered briefly about Verloff's obsession for cash. True, cash was featureless, and in the form of gold dust almost impossible to trace. Even gold bullion could be melted and recast. Perhaps the man's motives were rooted deep in the past. Whatever they

117

were, they had led the Pole out on a limb. He was committed for $60,000 for Stoneman's Inn and $40,-000 for Anchor, a cool hundred thousand. And if he had XL in mind, that would surely mean another $80,000.

The bait that would be dangled before Verloff's acquisitive eyes would cover that and more. Lark and Tetrault had arranged with Anderson for a leak of information, indicating the delayed shipment would be a quarter of a million. Not far off the real article, considering the long hiatus in gold shipments, and the production of the Bear mines. But to spring the trap, and catch large rats as well as small mice, everything must be brought into a complex whole at exactly the right time.

So the wide resources of the Agency were being marshaled to cover every eventuality. Everything must be placed as neatly as chessmen on a board, at Box B and Rail Fence, at Magma and Mantoul and Fort Ruskin, and especially at Stoneman's Gap and in Dead Man's Canyon. It was Lark's obligation to move the pieces in the opening gambit, then set his other pieces in motion, his bishops and rooks, his knights and pawns. And across the board was the king who must be brought to checkmate.

And the queen? Lark shook his head. He had no doubts about the role and the guilt of Sascha Verloff. But there were depths in the lovely Sonya he still had not plumbed. He still had the unwelcome thought she might be the brains behind this tremendously ambitious scheme. But even as he thought of it, he remembered the sobbing elegy of a rich violin on the hillside above two new-made graves. Could such a tender and selfless gesture come from a girl who had made murder an instrument of power?

That's the hell of this kind of work, Lark thought angrily. It isn't the first time—there was that little schoolteacher I left crying at Cobo Wells, with the man she was to marry dangling from a gallows in Cobo Town. There were four children left without father or mother at Walkerville, when the parents tried to outgun the guards at the bank, guards alerted by my tip. And that pretty Mexican señorita I left forlorn

118

and abandoned at Genesee Flats, her father and her brother and her lover rotting in prison because of what she had whispered to me in the dark passion of a summer night. Lark, you're a scoundrel! he told himself. Ah, but the game, the challenge—all else is secondary. Truth nor chivalry nor love must stand in the way of loyalty to the Agency. I'll break away, I'll quit, he vowed, to live my own life, a quiet warm life with a girl like Rimi Woodford, or a life full of surprise, gay and adventurous, with a Sonya Verloff. But even as he thought it, he wondered if he ever would.

He stood up and stared at himself in the mirror. An ugly fellow, he thought, though with clear eyes, good teeth, a rather pleasant smile. An ordinary fellow, though today he took a man's life. He was alive, and now he's dead. Damn the justification, that doesn't signify—am I taking on the prerogatives of God, that I can twitch my trigger finger and send a man to hell?

"Forget it, Lark, forget it!" he told himself fiercely, and turned away. He had a job, and come hell or high water, it was up to him to get it done. Afterwards there would be time enough to wax philosophical. He could assess the mental and moral cost of his actions. Then he could find satisfaction in the good lives of good people preserved and made safe again. If he could free one person from the hell of living in dread —but that satisfaction was for another day. Today he had killed a man.

He pulled the two harmless fangs of the empty shell casings from the S. & W. and replaced them. He cleaned the gun and restored it to the holster. Then he picked up the gunbelt from the bed and slowly buckled it around his middle, donning once again the tools of his deadly trade.

The leaves of the wild cucumber vines made a dappled pattern of shade on the veranda floor outside the parlor at Stoneman's Inn. Settees and sofas had been swung around near the French doors to form a horseshoe. Six men and one woman were seated there. They seemed uneasy in each other's presence, some patient, some nervous.

Lark looked at his watch for the dozenth time. Then his head came up and he pulled the lace curtains aside. "Here he is now," he said, satisfaction in his voice, and the seventh man joined them.

Lark took charge. "Friends, if you haven't met him, this is Art Rankine. Art, you know Con Tetrault, of course, and Miss Rimi Woodford. Ted Collins, our man in Fort Ruskin, and Kleberg, Loucks, and Nordstrom, assigned by our Denver office for the duration of the job."

As handshakes were exchanged, Rimi said with a smile, "The only person missing is Aunt Susan."

Lark propped the picture he had brought with him in place on a table. "The old gal is here in spirit, anyhow," he said. "So now, lady and gentlemen, to our council of war." He turned to Rankine. "You understand, Art, that this is war? Only the seven of us in this room are in the know on it, and if even a whisper goes beyond these walls, some of us may die."

Rankine nodded. "Can't take any chances in a deal as big as this must be. I ain't surprised you Pinkertons are in on it; I figured Bear Consolidated wasn't going to put up with the Redtops for much longer."

"We have some other clients, too," Lark said. "But that isn't material to our purpose. Con warned you about maintaining secrecy?"

"He did, and I haven't said a word to a living soul."

"Not to Ben Parchman? Not to your wife?"

"Wife's a luxury I can't afford," the marshal said with a grin. "As for Parchman, him and me don't jibe so I wouldn't give him the time of day. He's honest, though, the ornery old coot."

"You're positive of that? Good. But Art, we believe you've got a problem closer to home—we are pretty sure your man Flaherty is tied in with the Redtops, at least as an informer."

Rankine's jaw set hard. "The hell! I never put it past Frank to pocket a little legitimate graft, but the Redtops . . ."

"I think his tastes have proven too expensive for his salary," Lark said. "He's a boozefighter and a gambler, as you know, Art. He's been seen by Con talking to

Pike Sumter several times, and a little trap Con set resulted in Flaherty riding up the Box B road."

"It ain't much to hang a man on," Rankine said. "But I won't gainsay you, Lark. I've been a bit suspicious in the back of my mind about the way Frank blasted Clyde Prettiman."

"Clyde might have talked out of turn?"

"Right. And Frank followed somebody's orders to shut his mouth. I'll never quit digging into that bank robbery, and something Clyde dropped got around to me . . ." He went silent, looking off toward the depths of the canyon. He said, "Well, when I get back I'll hand him his walking papers, the son-of-a-bitch—pardon my French, Miss Rimi."

"No, no, Art, leave him alone," Lark said. "We want the Redtops tipped off to something. And the messenger will be Pike Sumter or Frank Flaherty. We're counting on it."

"I'm beginning to see the pitch. Give me the rest of it."

"As Con set it up with you, Anderson, of Bear Consolidated, will engage you to get three other trusted men and take the gold cleanup shipment to Mantoul. The word will get around that it contains two hundred and fifty thousand in bullion. You'll celebrate Anderson's well-paying commission by getting mildly drunk—you do take a drink, don't you?—and you'll drop enough to Flaherty for him to pass along. You'll spill the amount of the gold, and that you'll use a light wagon, with four guards besides the driver. Most important, you'll let him know the date—you'll be leaving at dawn July twenty-fifth or twenty-sixth. And that's all he'll be able to pump you for."

"And he'll pass it along to the big man? Good enough, I guess I can play drunk convincingly enough for that. Damn! I hate to think of Frank being on the crook. But I wouldn't lie to you, it doesn't surprise me a hell of a lot. Lessee now, July twenty-fifth, plenty of time to set your trap."

"Art, that's the date we want them to hear. Actually, the shipment will leave at dawn on the twenty-fourth. We'll drop that new time to the Redtops at the last minute."

Rankine stared at Lark, then his sharp features were illuminated by a smile. "Keep him off balance, eh, make him scramble? Move before he's ready—not bad, Lark, not bad. By the way, who is our man?"

Lark shook his head. "We've got some ideas, but no proof. We trust you, Art, but what you don't know won't hurt you, if this whole deal should blow up in our faces. No offense?"

"No offense," Rankine agreed. "You'll keep me posted on the final go-round?"

"Through Con or myself, Art. I may be riding with you as one of the four guards. I'll tell you one thing— if you help us pull this off, the Pinkerton National Detective Agency can be mighty generous to its friends."

Rankine looked at Lark squarely, his eyes narrowed. "Hell with that, Lark. God knows I hate a squealer or a stool pigeon. But I'd turn both if we can bring an end to this murderous gang. They're plumb ruining the whole country, and you can count on me to help bust 'em wide open once and for all."

"Good man," Lark said, laying a hand on the smaller man's shoulder. "Rimi, have you got that dummy package they sent up from Mantoul? That's your cover for coming to the Gap this morning. Be sure that Flaherty sees it before you deliver it to Anderson. Hint that it is so valuable Anderson sent you here to pick it up in person."

Rimi Woodford handed Rankine the shoebox-sized package, wrapped in heavy brown paper, and with every cross of its cords locked in sealing wax imprinted with the Bear Consolidated insigne. Rankine hefted it. "Sure looks impressive enough," he said. "Anything of real value in it?"

"A dozen starched linen collars, size fifteen and a half," Lark told him. "Bill Anderson's size."

Rankine shrugged. "Well, they're damned scarce in this neck o' the woods, which might make 'em valuable, all right. Lark, you'll see to tailing the Magma informant?"

"It's all set up, don't worry about it. There's another thing to worry about, though—Art, as captain of

122

the gold escort, it's damned likely you'll get shot at, even though we do all we can to copper that bet."

"It wouldn't be the first time I smelled powder smoke, or had bullets buzz round my ears," Rankine said. "I'll take my chances, and get a shot or two back at 'em."

Lark and the others watched the marshal as he went through the French doors and tied the package behind the saddle of his waiting horse. He mounted, and scanned roads and terrain carefully before he rode off toward Magma, with a wave of the hand.

"Looks like a good man. Glad he's on our side," Kleberg said.

"He is," Lark confirmed. "An ace in the hole the Redtops don't know we have."

They went over the plans again, with intense concentration, adding refinements, posting assignments, checking the all-important timing. Lark was satisfied when the meeting broke up, shortly before the arrival of the Mantoul stage.

When he walked with Rimi to the lobby, she said, "Justin, Marsh Bailor has come and I've put him to work. He's taking over most of the stable chores from Phil. I'm not sure I was wise to hire him before this other thing was over."

"It's all right, Rimi. What did you think of him?"

"I had a long straight talk with him, and he took it well. But I thought this morning the boy seemed depressed, and sort of angry, short-tempered."

"I'm sure there's nothing to worry about," Lark said. "But if you'll send Lolly out, I'll see if she knows anything."

A moment after Rimi had disappeared through the swinging door into the kitchen, Lolly Bailor came out, wiping her floury hands on her apron. She looked distraught, the dusting of freckles on her face standing out like copper pennies. She asked with some hesitation, "You wanted to see me, Mr. Lark?"

"Lolly, I'm sure you are pleased that Miss Rimi has taken Marsh on. But she says he's acting rather strangely."

"I guess he got upset when he learned that Lippy was dead, and that you—you shot Lippy."

123

"You tell Marsh it was Lippy or me, though I'm sure he knows that already. I thought Marsh, like you, didn't care much for the other brothers."

She nodded slowly. "That's right. Only Lippy—well, he was family, and to get shot dead—I ain't sayin' he didn't have it coming, Mr. Lark. But Marsh—well, he's young and confused, Mr. Lark. He'll come around."

"He'd better," Lark said, rather harshly. "If the kid blows this chance with Miss Rimi, no telling where he'll end up."

"I know. But paw and Anse and Buzz and Lippy, they was always talking big and stupid about 'the pride of the Bailors.' They didn't have no more real pride than hogs rootin' in the mud of their sty, but they talked big. And I guess some of that rubbed off on Marsh."

"He'd do well to forget that buncombe," Lark said. "You talk to him, Lolly. Tell him he's his own man now, it's up to him to think for himself."

"I'll do that, Mr. Lark. Why is it that when men are young, they never seem to think, just go rammin' ahead like bulls, whether they're right or wrong?"

Lark laughed. " 'Twas ever thus, my little old lady of nineteen. Now run along, and leave your problems to Miss Rimi or me. Quit making your pretty head ache with them."

"I wish I could," she said darkly, and hurried away.

Lark watched her go, hearing the faint tinkle of a warning bell in the back of his mind. The girl's life at Box B had made her wary. She could scent trouble as a wild animal tests the wind. And Lark felt it too, the very air of Stoneman's Gap heavy and ominous, sharp with the smell of brimstone. The jangle of alarm was winding up the scale like the tightening strings of his guitar.

This was not a new feeling to Lark. Whenever a big case was approaching its climax, he was stirred by this same excitement, a quickening rush and thrust that made him preternaturally alert, and lifted by a tingling electricity into the clearest exactitude of thought. He was moved by stirrings of prescience, and often at such times his hunches struck the mark beyond the normal permutations of luck.

124

In one of their talks Lark had tried to describe to Rimi this exhilaration of danger, this stimulus of mind and nerve and muscle. She had nodded, but he had not been sure that she truly understood. He wondered if Sonya would not come closer to sharing the lift of it, aye, the thrill of danger breathing hot on the nape of the neck. Sonya had the sensitivity of the musician, an instinctive reaction to nuances of feeling sometimes missed by more prosaic souls. Lark felt an edge of chill at the thought—would this perceptivity of the Polish girl bring her a foreknowledge of her brother's impending peril? Lark doubted if the strong-willed Sascha would heed any such psychic warning. But Lark determined to watch his thoughts as well as his words through every second of his few remaining days at Rail Fence Ranch.

He was standing on the inn porch when the Mantoul coach came rumbling out of the cleft of Dead Man's Canyon and stopped by the steps in a clatter of noise. Phil Woodford and another young man came hurrying through the front door to meet the stage.

Lark said, "Hi, Phil. Hello, Marsh. How goes it?"

"Hi, Mr. Lark," Phil Woodford said, with a wide smile. But Marsh Bailor did not speak. He gave Lark a cold glance, then turned his head aside as he strode past. Frowning, Lark looked after the boy and shook his head sadly.

12

Rail Fence Ranch
July 23, 1887

Dear Aunt Susan:

Bound for Magma on business for Mr. Verloff. Will mail this at Stoneman's Gap as I go through. All plans made; we are all busy and have hired extra help. A market tip—I think Bear Consolidated stock will be going up. Take care of yourself and DON'T WORRY.

Your aff. nephew,
Justin

◄◄◄◄◄◄◄◄◄◄◄◄◄◄◄◄◄◄◄◄◄◄◄◄◄◄◄◄◄◄

Lark was sitting on the shaded porch of the mansion at Rail Fence, softly picking out a tune on his guitar, a tune which had been running through his head but which he could not place. Behind him the last searchlights of the setting sun were flaming the dour peaks of the Running Wolfs across the valley as footlights flood a stage. A cool swirl of air thrust at the heavy heat of the day, carrying the smell of new-cut hay and the tang of woodsmoke. The ranch sounds came clear and plain; from the barn came the doleful moo of a dairy cow protesting the injustice of life.

Perversely, though his plans would erupt into violence in the next forty-eight hours, Lark was calm and at peace with the world. Today's meeting had gone smoothly. Now there was no turning back, his die was cast. He was immersed in a frame of mind philosophical and fatalistic. If the plan went well, fine; if it was thrown awry by events he had not foreseen, why then, he would shift his objectives in the very middle of furious action. Why should a man worry? Worry brought gray hairs, and a contraction of the solar plexus into painful knots.

So as the muted notes of his guitar lifted light on the evening breeze, Lark's speculation touched just as lightly on the single unknown factor which troubled him—Sonya Verloff. He was still unable to resolve her guilt or her innocence, the extent of her inner knowledge and her culpability. She was still an intriguing mystery to Lark, as mysterious as she had been the first evening he had met her.

He knew, and recoiled a little at the knowing, that he had broken one of the prime rules of the Pinkerton operative—he had become personally involved with a suspect. Sonya Verloff had a magnetism for him deeper than any woman he had ever known. For the mutable facets of her nature he found answers, and then found the answers wrong. He sensed that under her immense charm, she had an underlying strength beyond that of many women. The same strength, he thought, that Rimi Woodford has, but with Rimi, it is a known strength for good. But is Sonya's strength a power for good, or for evil? Still far from an answer, he shook his head.

The tune came to him then, and his fingers worked out its rhythm. Softly he put words to it, " 'Twas way out in New Mexico. along the Spanish line, I was workin' for old Clayton Boone, a man well past his prime. Well he rides in and asks of me, 'What's happened to my lady?' I says to him, 'She's quit your range . . .' "

A footstep beside him startled him into silence, and his hand swept the pick across the strings in a jangle of sound. When he looked up, Sonya Verloff was smiling at him. She said, "My, what a sad song! Eet is like ze sad ballads we sing in Poznan, which people like me enjoy ver' much to cry about."

"The song is called 'Clayton Boone,' " Lark said. "But before American cowboys latched onto it, it was a tune in Scotland centuries old called 'The Gypsy Laddie.' Cowboys, you know, love slow sad tunes to sing when they ride night herd."

With a sweep of her skirts, Sonya took a seat beside him. "Do not let me stop you, Justin. My mood tonight is also ver' sad."

"What's the trouble, Sonya?" he asked.

She shrugged, a graceful and expressive shrug. "I could not tell you, Justin. Sascha and I, we have ze Russian blood, you know. Ze Russian, he can be sad for no reason, ver' ver' sad. But I think—I have ze feeling . . ." Her voice dwindled, and she stared out at the flare of the dying sunset on the harsh rock of the mountains. Watching her, Lark saw more than sadness in her chiseled face. There was a shadow of dread upon it, of a terror beyond the moment. For the first time, Lark thought he had been given a glimpse of the real woman under that lovely mask.

He struck his pick to the strings of his guitar and

127

began a simply lively tune with a rhythm that set the head nodding and the toes tapping. He sang softly, "I ride an ol' paint, I'm leadin' ol' Dan, I'm headin' for Montan' for to throw the houlihan . . ." Head bent over the instrument, he went through three verses, and stopped with a thrust of the hand.

She laughed delightedly, a laugh of genuine amusement. "You play well, Justin. In your music I can hear ze hoofs of ze horses as zey lope along ze steep trail. Already you make me feel not so—w'at you say?— down in ze dumps."

"I'm glad. A pretty girl like you should never be sad," he said. "I'll have to teach you some of these cowboy ballads, Sonya—these are the music of our wide, bold land."

She gave him an intense look with something of a question in it. She said, "That would be ver' fine, Justin, if ze land is not swept by fire and ze big blue sky do not fall. Justin, I am sad once again, I haff again ze doubt and ze uncertainty of life. I am giving too much thought to . . ."

The screen door swung closed with a muted slam, and Lark turned to see Sascha Verloff approaching. He was the picture of the storied gentleman, in silk smoking jacket and striped trousers, cordovan slippers on his feet and a silk Ascot at his throat. He's not his usual suave self, Lark thought; he looks annoyed, and petulant, and with a hint of suppressed anger.

With a jerk of the head he said to Sonya, "It is getting cool out here, my dear. I think you had better go inside. You must avoid any possibility of lung complaint . . ."

She stood up quickly, herself annoyed. "Sascha, you know I have ze constitution of ze peasant, and never in my life have ze lungs or ze cough bothered me. If you want to talk business with Justin, why do you not say so? But I go, I go."

With a graceful stride, and an uncompromising straight set of her back, she left them. The screen door swung shut behind her. Verloff dropped into the chair she had vacated.

128

"Disturbing news just came, Lark," he said. "You noticed the man who rode in a bit ago?"

"I saw the son-of-a-bitch. Anse Bailor, wasn't it?"

"Yes, one of my less reliable hangers-on, but a necessary messenger. Lark, his news requires a change of plan."

"Since you've never confided your plans to me, I doubt I can be of much help," Lark said pointedly.

"I know. I have been secretive, but you must understand I am a man who keeps his own counsel, Lark," Verloff said. "I order the world to my own pattern. I would soon have told you my plan to have you direct a certain operation, but now circumstances dictate that I must direct it myself. You will have another assignment, one of great danger. Will you accept it?"

Lark stared at Verloff, his eyes cold. "Mister, I'm ready for anything that has a profit to it. I came to Rail Fence because I thought you could provide that. I'm ready."

"You think you have solved my blueprint, my master plan?"

"Most of it, and I want in. You've been empire-building, Verloff. On other people's money. It was your fertile brain which conceived the Redtop operations, and saw that they were carried out with success, and a minimum of risk, with Rod Starbolt as your tool. Now you've made more heavy commitments, Stoneman's Inn, the Anchor ranch, and God knows what else. And I think, Mr. Sascha Verloff, that you have a scheme to get the wherewithal to cover those commitments—again someone else's money."

"You come damned close to knowing too much, Lark," Verloff said icily. "How did you come by this?"

"I added the numbers, Verloff. I've been in big and fast and deadly games before, I know the run of the cards. Don't get the idea I'm objecting, mister. I know you need me, I know I can cut the buck. But I'll want my share of the loot, and a fat share."

"You do the job the way I want it done, and you won't be disappointed at the reward. You've got the brains, something Starbolt lacked. Oh, he was a satisfactory tool in the early stages. But when he started to think, he lost his usefulness." Standing up, Verloff walked to the railing and stared out for a long minute toward the mountains. He came back and sat down again. He put a hand on Lark's knee.

"Lark, I'm convinced you are the man I need. I guessed that when I first saw you, and after Denver confirmed your record—well, my plans took an ambitious leap. With me to plan, Lark, and you to execute, there's no limit to the possibilities. We can put the whole country in our pockets, from the Canadian line to that park they call the Yellowstone. Banks, Lark, ranches, stage and freight lines, sheep and cattle and mining—all ours, Lark, if we play it right. Montana will be a state soon—we'll pad the legislature with our men. The crooks we'll pay off, the idealists we'll tease with the carrot of success. Why, the governor, the judges, everyone from the top down to the county sheriffs, we'll own every man jack of them! A gold mine, Lark, waiting to be stripped clean. You and I will own it from top to bottom, a whole state, Lark! Imagine it."

"You're plainly a man of vision, Verloff," Lark said slowly. "But as for our association—I'm not so sure. Some of your methods bother me, they're too dangerous. This banditry is risky as all hell. How much safer to have worked through the banks and the money changers; they do their stealing legally. With your brains you could have worked the con on them, and never risked a thing. The other way, your way, has the shadow of the gallows looming black across it."

"I have my reasons, and I have the law in my pocket."

"That's as may be," Lark said. "But the ordinary citizens of any region will stand for only so much. Beyond that—why, they'll band together, and court or no court, law or no law, they'll hang you and all your men higher than Haman. I've seen signs already that vigilante law isn't far removed."

"I'm neither blind nor stupid, Lark," Verloff said. "That's one reason I had to—uh, dispose of Starbolt. His excesses were turning the country against us, against me."

130

"It was Starbolt killed the two Woodfords? And Sheriff Martin?"

"Regrettably, yes. He gravely exceeded my orders. There were other ways, but Starbolt knew only one. You see, Lark, by the purest of accident, the Woodfords had learned of evidence which connected me with the Redtops. They managed to pass it along to the sheriff when he was—uh, unfortunately drowned. After that my man Starbolt became more and more independent. My plans, Lark, cannot tolerate an ambitious man. So Starbolt had to go."

"My point remains the same, Verloff. This operation without the law will prove fatal in the long run. You can antagonize the common people only so long. If I go in with you, I want your assurance that we'll find a better way to finance the deal than by banditry."

"Of course, my own ideas exactly. Lark, I have a pool of money in Europe I can tap—relatives, investors, greedy dupes. I obtained one sum of eighty-five thousand that I used to great advantage. Six months ago an amount of two hundred thousand dollars in Polish funds was on its way here, and I had committed it. Then my emissary skipped with it and fled to Rome." He looked at Lark with a penetrating glance that had a touch of threat in it. "That messenger, Lark, didn't live to spend much of my money. He was found in the Tiber with both hands cut off and twenty-seven stab wounds in his body. Which of course did not get my money back, but I feel it may be a salutary lesson to any man who tries to doublecross Sascha Verloff."

"There's still a reservoir of cash in Europe?" Lark asked.

"Bottomless, sir, bottomless. But any transfer is a long and involved process. The loss of that two hundred thousand proved very embarrassing, with commitments to meet. You see, Lark, a tragic experience in my youth—it is my inexorable rule not to borrow, unless I own the bank myself. Which I will, of course, in time. But not yet. So to meet these commitments, Lark, I must marshal the famous Redtop gang in one profitable final coup. Then the gang will vanish forever into limbo and legend. But I need this final pay-off. As it must not fail, I'll direct it myself."

"And my part in this coup?"

"If we had more time, you would be my good right hand. But since we have not, you will be one of my victims."

Lark looked at him, startled. "How's that again?"

Verloff chuckled, and took his time selecting and lighting a cigar. "Lark, do you know Art Rankine?"

"The marshal of Magma? A little. I got acquainted with him when I was driving the shuttle stage. We never got very friendly, because I was always uncomfortable in the presence of an honest man."

"Your guess was good; Rankine is totally honest. Which plays into our hands. From a source in Rankine's confidence, I have learned that because of this honesty of his, he has been chosen to captain the guard contingent when Bear Consolidated ships its next gold cleanup from Magma to Mantoul. That gold bullion, Lark, amounts to a quarter of a million dollars. I intend to take it away from Rankine in Dead Man's Canyon. Since the man and the others with him will be tough and dangerous and incorruptible, it will be your task to be one of them."

"To help take them out from the inside?" Lark asked. "Well, I guess it could be done. A lot of ifs to it."

"There are," Verloff said, blowing blue smoke at the ragged streaks of the fading sunset. "And we have no time to waste. My first word was that the shipment would not leave Magma until the twenty-fifth at the earliest. Now the Magma man—my informer, that is —says they will leave the twenty-fourth, at dawn."

"Time's short. How can I convince Rankine between now and then that I'm the man to ride with him?"

"It's quite simple—you will tell Rankine that you've heard there will be an attempt to steal the gold, so you have to ride along with the shipment."

"And what is my excuse to Rankine for that?"

"Because you are an operative of the Pinkerton National Detective Agency, assigned to the Redtop case." Verloff was smiling.

Lark's head snapped up. "Me? A cop? That's a lot of cow chips, Verloff. You must be joshing."

"Give it a little thought, man. Rankine has been heard to say he was surprised the Bear people hadn't brought the Pinkertons in before this. He'll fall for it. And what better cover is there?"

Lark nodded thoughtfully, not revealing that the shock of Verloff's surprising statement had been all too genuine. He said, "What if Rankine checks with the Bear manager, Anderson?"

"You've been sent there by Bear's Mantoul office, under cover even to the local manager. Why Lark, it's a dead immortal cinch. You ride to Magma tomorrow, you talk to Rankine, and you'll be one of the guards the next morning. I'll guarantee it."

"And at the right time I'll throw down on Rankine and his men and disarm them? Well, it ought to work, if I can get Rankine to take me. Where will you hit the treasure wagon?"

"Remember the holdup you were in? The same place, an ideal ambush. Men call it 'The Slot.' "

"And the time?"

"About eleven in the morning. And Lark, I think you had better dispose of Rankine. And his men."

Lark stared at him. "Kill them, you mean?"

Verloff nodded. He said, his tone matter of fact, "Yes. You will be riding out of Magma by daylight, without disguise. The Redstone races past the Slot in a welter of spray, the water as wild as a bucking bronco. Later the river maybe will give up some dead bodies, even four of them. But it will not be surprising if yours is never found."

"So I disappear," Lark said. "And then?"

"Anse and Buzz Bailor will take us over the back trails, beyond the canyon walls. We'll come back here unseen. Then a change of mustache, a different haircut, a pair of steel-rimmed glasses, and you become Gordon Lark, brother of the unfortunate man who was lost in the holdup of the gold shipment."

"By God, Verloff, you're a dandy!" Lark exclaimed. "Got it figured out to the last detail, eh? Pack horses to load with the gold, I suppose. And then men,

133

horses, gold, all disappear into thin air. A stroke of genius, that's what it is, genius."

For a second Lark thought he might have been spreading it on too thick, but then he saw that Verloff was lapping it up as a tomcat laps cream. Here is a man completely satisfied with himself, Lark thought. He has been playing with life and death so long he imagines he is God.

He stood up, the guitar still on the neck strap. "Just one thing, boss," he said. "Why are you so hell-bent on getting your hands on Stoneman's Inn?"

Verloff came to his feet, tossing his half-smoked cigar out into the yard. He clapped Lark on the shoulder. "Half the country has guessed at the reason, but only Sascha Verloff knows. It did cost me a liberal bribe in a certain Chicago office, but it was worth it. Lark, the Great Pacific has scouted a route for a railroad from the main line at Mantoul to Fort Ruskin, and perhaps on to Canada. There are three possible routes through the Running Wolfs. The Great Pacific engineers have chosen the easiest and best—Dead Man's Canyon."

Lark whistled softly. "Not just the Inn, then, but that fine bottom land beyond it—another of your gold mines, Verloff."

"Exactly. There, Mr. Justin Lark, will rise the flourishing community called Verloff City, shortly to become the metropolis of western Montana. And every stick and stone of it, Lark, every street and alley, its land and its water, its grass and its trees, every stick and stone of it will be mine, Lark, mine."

13

Magma, M.T.
July 24, 1887

Dear Aunt Susan:

In haste—leaving in a few minutes for Mantoul with the treasure wagon. All plans complete, all men in place. All we can do now is keep our powder dry—and pray a little. Will wire you a complete report of results as soon as feasible. Take care of yourself and keep your fingers crossed for us.

Your aff. nephew,

Justin

The rising sun was painting the snowfields of the Running Wolf peaks with gold as the treasure wagon turned from the Magma lane into the Pioneer Creek road. There was little unusual in the appearance of the vehicle, a light Studebaker, its box green, the wheels red-striped. It was drawn by a team of fine draft horses. Above the regular wagon box rose an enclosed express body without windows, its front and side panels extended at the front so the driver was protected from weather and almost concealed from view except from directly ahead.

When the wagon had topped the first long hill and dropped down the slope beyond into the trees, Lark spurred his Mingus mule alongside the team and raised a hand. "All right, Val," he said to Kleberg, the driver. "Here's a good spot to get organized. We'll turn the reins over to Raghead Willie from here on out."

Kleberg grinned and halted the team. He jumped down to join Lark, Rankine, Collins, and Tetrault, who had dismounted. They walked to the rear of the wagon, and Lark unlatched the double doors and pulled them open.

It was evident then that the wagon was not as innocent a conveyance as it had appeared to be. A great deal of work had been put into it in the Robbins and Tucker stables at Magma, under the supervision of Rankine and Tetrault. Gimpy the hostler had guarded the secrecy of the work with the zeal of pent-up hate, for his K-leg was the result of a Redtop bullet in an early holdup. And the blacksmith who had done most of the work was the brother of a man killed by the Redtops. There had been no interference from Ben Parchman, the line manager, for he prided himself on being an executive, above the mundane details of horseflesh and harness and manure. So the stables seldom if ever saw him.

The blacksmith had plated the floor and the roof and the four sides with steel thick enough to turn a rifle bullet. There were firing slots in each direction, cleverly concealed by ornamentation, provided with covers which could be locked in place until firepower was needed. At the front above the seat, a slit had been cut for vision, and below it was a narrow opening by which the reins could be extended to the interior. Two men were riding inside, on makeshift cushions of gunnysacking.

The verisimilitude had been carried out even to the shipment. Small wooden boxes, piled tightly, were banded with steel strapping. Each was marked WESTERN TERRITORIAL BANK, Mantoul, M.T. The boxes were heavy, as a quarter-million in gold bullion would be. But they contained ingots of lead, masked with a wash of gilt.

"Let's put him to work," Lark said. Fred Loucks and Robbie Nordstrom lifted an inert figure and passed him to the men at the tailgate of the wagon. Lark and Val Kleberg carried the figure to the front of the wagon and boosted it to the seat. Concealed clamps

136

went around the thighs and middle, the leather reins were slipped through the hands and through a slot in the steel armor. Lark adjusted the hat on the head, straightened the shoulders, and patted Willie on the cheek. "Hang tough, kid," he said, and jumped to the ground, dusting his hands.

"Damned if Raghead doesn't look real enough to talk," Rankine said admiringly. "Think he'll fool the Redtops?"

Tetrault cocked his head, studying the dummy. "I'd bet on it. He'll be in the shadow of the extended sides and canopy. And that gang is nervous on the trigger finger; they'll shoot first and start thinking later, if at all."

"He's a work of art," Lark added. "Con, you and Rimi must have had fun building him."

"It was crazy," Tetrault said, grinning. "Say, that's some girl, Justin, that Rimi. The way she keeps that place running in spite of everything, and can still give a man a smile. It was Rimi's idea to give Raghead Willie that mustache. She insisted it had to be neat and narrow—just like Lark's, she said."

"He looks like me all right," Lark said. "And I'm not sure we don't have the same kind of brain. Val, you can drive the team all right from the inside?"

"We tried it out last night in Magma, with Fred in the front seat instead of Willie. Went all right, no trouble."

"Good. Then let's go—Val and Fred and Robbie inside; Art, Ted and Con and me will ride shotgun with you. Be ready, with a shell jacked into the chamber. They might hit us anywhere—I don't put much faith in what our Polish friend told me."

Rankine swung up into the saddle. "So it's Verloff," he said. "Can't say I'm surprised. The grapevine has carried rumors about him now and again. But he's a clever son-of-a-bitch; he got a good cover, and uses it."

"He's out from under it this time," Lark said, his tone grim. "All right, boys, let's be on our way."

He and Rankine moved into the point position, ahead of the wagon. Rankine gestured. "Fresh tracks. Our friend Pike Sumter. I saw him ride out, hell-bent."

137

"To pass the word we're coming. What about Flaherty?"

"Sitting on his duff in the Rank and File, thinkin' how he'll spend his cut. I did some checking on him, Lark, and you were right; he's in it up to his bat ears. I'll take care of him when I get back, and he ain't going to like it."

At the weathered sign that read *Box B* they saw the fresh tracks of a dozen horses, coming from the north and turning up Barber Creek before the dew had misted from the long grass. "A dozen or so," Lark said, surveying the hoofprints. "They've got to move right along if they're coming over the ridge into Dead Man's. Lolly told me that trail is plain hell for steep."

"Been me, I'd have gone straight up the main road," Rankine said. "But that wouldn't fit in with Verloff's habit of covering up every angle. He knows he don't own the country yet."

"But he aims to, Art," Lark said. "He damn well aims to."

The wagon with its outriders reached Stoneman's Gap without incident. Lark said, "Art, take the wagon past the inn to the notch of the canyon. Con and I will bring up the fresh team. We don't want Raghead Willie talking to anyone."

To Lark's surprise, it was Rimi who was waiting at the stables with the fresh team. She handed the halter ropes to Lark. "I'll go along and bring back the other team," she said.

"Come up here, then," Tetrault said. He reached down a powerful arm, and with a swing, levered her up to a seat astride behind his saddle. She smiled at him, not perturbed by her unladylike display of lovely legs as her skirts hiked up. She put an arm around Tetrault's waist. "Let's go, Con," she said, and Lark's eyebrows lifted sardonically, as he saw that he was left to bring along the team.

As Kleberg and Collins changed the teams, Rimi slid down from Tetrault's horse. "Thanks, Con," she said. "I'll ride back on one of the draft horses." She looked up at Lark. "Justin, something has happened that I don't like. It may not mean a thing, but a short time ago Phil saw Marsh Bailor ride east toward the canyon on that calico pony of his."

"You think he was armed?"

"Phil said Marsh had a rifle. Phil wanted to follow him, but I wouldn't let him."

"Good girl," Lark said. He mulled over the significance of this new development, frowning. Then reaching down, he patted the girl's shoulder. "Rimi, don't worry about it. We'll watch for him, but there isn't much he can do at this stage of the game."

"I guess not, but all this—it scares me, Justin," she said. Tetrault was standing beside her, and to Lark's surprise the girl reached out to hold tight the hand of his partner. "I guess I'm being stupid, but I worry about that little fool getting into trouble as if it were one of my two kids."

"You ask Lolly about it?" Lark asked.

"She's worried too. The boy has been moody ever since he learned you had killed Lippy. He has it in for you, she says."

"A bad move could get him killed, the way things are," Lark said. "Well, it will all be over in the next couple of hours. Then we can pick up the pieces. Wish us luck, Rimi."

She stared at him, eyes wide, then her glance turned toward Tetrault. "I'll do more than that, I'll pray for all of you," she said. "If anything should happen to you, Justin, or to Con, or—or any of you, it would be terrible. I couldn't stand it." There were tears in those fine blue eyes.

"We'll be careful," Lark said. "And Rimi, you and your people be alert. Keep your guns at hand. There may be stragglers, and if so, they could be desperate men."

"I'm a good shot, and so is Phil," she said, determination in her voice. "We'll be on the lookout. After the stage from Fort Ruskin pulls in at three o'clock, we'll have other folks around."

"Good enough. And listen, if they steal any horses, just let them go. We'll settle that later. Maybe I should leave Con here just in case."

She shook her head. "You haven't any more men now than you need. We'll be all right. Oh, I hate all this—hate it!" She stood with the halter ropes of the team in her hands, the tears streaming unheeded down her cheeks.

"We've got to go, baby," Tetrault said. "Here." He boosted her to the back of one of the horses. She gave him a shaky smile and drummed her heels into the ribs of the horse. Leading the other, she rode off down the road toward the stables.

Tetrault, watching her, said, "I don't like that, Justin—about young Bailor, I mean."

"No more do I. But I didn't want to frighten Rimi with it," Lark said. "Let's you and I take a scout well ahead. Art, keep our wagon moving at a fast clip. If we run into anything we'll circle back."

Lark's mule and Tetrault's horse moved at a canter into the jaws of Dead Man's Canyon, the hoofbeats drumming an echo in the rocky walls. The air had been heavy with the heat of late July, but now it was cool, for the sun barely penetrated the high cliffs for a short time each day. With an analytical part of his mind not occupied with the present enterprise, Lark wondered what severe problems the Great Pacific might encounter trying to operate a railroad through this precipitous gap in winter—snow and ice, slides and high water.

They had gone two miles into the canyon, three, the broken stone clicking to the cadence of the hoofbeats. The river turned, and bent again, its flow now much diminished from the day Lark had first seen it from the stagecoach. It hissed over rocks which had been eddies in the racing flow, but were now wicked fangs festooned with white water, sharp teeth in the plunging swirl of the Redstone. As they passed, a fishing bird took alarm and rose with heavy flapping strokes to seek quieter terrain.

They rode around a sharp bend. In men like Justin Lark and Con Tetrault, who had been riding the danger trail for years, an instinct builds up, an expertise which is hard to describe or to explain, except that it exists. The recognition of peril did not require thought. Thus when Lark caught a momentary shine of metal behind a bush on the cliffside ahead, an instant reaction kneed the Mingus mule solidly against the flank of Tetrault's horse, and they went crashing off the roadway into the sparse fringe of brush.

From the road where they had been, a puff of dust spurted up. Ahead, powder smoke bloomed from behind the bush. The slam of the shot echoed back from the encompassing walls. Lark swung an arm, and on the signal Tetrault urged his horse sharply through the brush to the right. Lark slapped the Mingus on the flank, and the mule went surging along the edge of the road, quite understanding the urgency of the matter.

A second shot, and the bullet struck the rock wall behind Lark, the lead whining off into the distance like an angry wasp. Lark, beyond the purview of the marksman, dismounted and looped reins around a branch. Bending low, he scrambled through brush to the shoulder of the rocky bend. He found cover behind a protruding boulder. Not far to his right was the brush clump from which the shots had come.

Though the sniper could not see Tetrault, Lark could, finding him bellied down under cover, rifle in hand. Lark signaled, pointing toward the bush. Tetrault slashed three shots at the sniper's position as fast as he could work the lever. As the marksman returned the fire, Lark worked his way along the slope. He was only a few feet away, pistol in hand, when he called, "Drop the gun, Marsh. If you shoot, you're a dead man."

Marsh Bailor took one look at Lark, and despair on his face, stood up slowly. The rifle dropped from his grasp as his hands went up. He was not wearing a sidearm, so Lark holstered his own pistol. He jacked the shells out of the rifle and leaned it against a boulder. Hands on hips, he stared at Marsh. He shook his head.

"Youngster, I swear I can't understand you," he said. "You get a break, a good chance to clear away from that rotten family of yours, a job with Miss Rimi, and you blow it."

"I don't need no lecture," Marsh said sullenly. "Us Bailors is real tough hombres. We can take care of ourselves."

Tetrault came scrambling up the slope. At Marsh's

defiant words, Tetrault said, "You speak respectful to your elders, Bailor. Else I'll give you a quick one across the chops."

Lark raised a placating hand. "Hold it, Con. Let's see if we can't find out what this is all about."

"Damn you, you killed my brother," Marsh said. "Shot him down like a dog. I'm a Bailor, it's my task to get even."

Lark gave a sigh of exasperation. "Marsh, Marsh, what's the matter with you? You know your brother pulled down on me. On top of that, what did Lippy or any of them except Lolly ever do for you? Nothing, except to get you in trouble, work you, talk you into getting yourself killed. And for what?"

"It's my family. We gotta stick together."

"There it is again. Who's been feeding you this guff? Who gave you that tale about Lippy's death?"

"Buzz said . . ."

"Oh, it's Buzz, is it?" Lark snapped. "We're running out of time, Marsh. I want the straight story, and I want it now."

"Well, when I skun out from Box B, I taken my rifle and my six-gun. Last night Buzz sneaks down to the Gap, and into the bunkhouse where I stay. He said he had a big job today, hadda have my six, his was busted. I wouldn't give it to him until he tole me all about what he was up to. When I give it to him, and onst he had it, he cussed me out for a yellow-belly, because I hadn't done nothin' to you for killin' Lippy. Said you shot him down cold. Called me a stinkin' coward, and a lot of other stuff. He made me so mad I tole him I'd show him, I wasn't scairt, I'd take care of you today, for sure. So I tried."

"Kid, I guess knowing what to believe and what to discount comes with experience," Lark said. "Your brother is a stupid, lying tough, which you should know by this time. All this brag talk of his was just to get you into trouble as deep as his own."

"I guess maybe he wasn't steerin' me right," Marsh said.

"He was aiming to get you hung," Lark said. He watched as the young man, his head bowed, scuffed at the shale of the slope with a boot toe. Lark struck

142

the iron home. "Something you should know, kid. You're mighty fond of Lolly, aren't you? She ever tell you what made her finally leave home? This he-man brother of yours, Buzz, laid for her in the barn at Box B and tried to get her to give in to him. His own sister, mind you."

"Why, Goddamn him!" Marsh said harshly. He looked at Lark uncertainly. "You wouldn't lie to me, Mr. Lark?"

Lark shook his head. "Lolly told me herself."

Marsh drew a deep breath. "Then I guess I'll have to grow up some. Mr. Lark, he tole me he was riding with the Redtops today. But the holdup wouldn't be at the Slot, like everybody was made to think. The gang'll come over the mountain trail from Box B, and hold up the treasure wagon about three miles this side of the Slot, when nobody's expecting it. And Buzz and Anse and Pike Sumter, they got a special assignment. After they've got the guards, if me or somebody else ain't got you already, the three of them is to make sure that they kill you dead."

"Kill me? And why should they do that?"

"Because Mr. Big—Buzz wouldn't tell me who he is—says you're a Pinkerton detective, and he wants to make an example out of you. Buzz says when they're through, the agency will think twice about sending any more Pinks into Mr. Big's territory."

"I'll be damned," Lark said. He pushed back his Stetson and wiped sweat from his brow. "What else did he tell you?"

"He says when this raid is over, he'll have Mr. Big by the balls. He's gonna make the boss give him Stoneman's Inn when he's got it away from Miss Rimi, else he'll spill the beans to the U.S. marshal, all about the Redtops, and Mr. Big."

"He'll play hell, too," Lark said. "So you want to see Buzz steal the inn from Miss Rimi? What about your sister Lolly then? Come off it, Marsh. We're in a tight bind as it is."

"I been a damn fool, Mr. Lark. I wisht I could do something to make it right."

"You can, Marsh," Lark said. "Lolly told me you know this country better than anyone, even Buzz. I

143

want to cut around and get behind the Redtops after they come down the trail from Box B."

Marsh stared at the sheer cliff across the river, as if he were studying a picture in his mind. "It can be done, if we move fast. It's rougher'n all hell, and the last mile would have to be on foot."

"You'll guide us, kid? Good for you. Here comes the wagon now. Soon as I give them the dope we'll skin out."

Art Rankine's eyes were cold and angry as Lark told him quickly what he and Tetrault had learned from the boy. "You were right not to trust that conniving bastard, Lark," he said. "Not that we wouldn't have been ready, but that extra edge of surprise might have hurt. How you gonna work it?"

Lark rubbed his square jaw. His smile was bland. "Let's shake up their timetable," he said. "Art, you and the boys slow down to a walk. Instead of eleven o'clock at the Slot, we won't get three miles this side until noon. Meantime me and Con and Marsh will move up behind them." He glanced at the sun, frowning. "What d'you think?"

"I can see our Mr. V. and his Redtops getting nervous as the sun climbs higher," Rankine said. "But watch out for any outposts, Lark. They might string out some guards."

"I doubt it, they're shorthanded. But we'll be careful. We won't make a move from our side until someone drills Raghead Willie."

From the steel vault of the wagon came Val Kleberg's voice, almost sepulchral in its confinement. "Justin, I heard that new time, but for God's sake, don't stretch it any farther. If you do, me'n Fred and ol' Robbie will be cooked geese, ready for a fresh basting. It's hottern'n the hinges of hell in this tin cage."

"You'll find things hotter yet as soon as we hit the Redtops," Lark said. He hit the outer panel with the heel of his hand, making the steel plate boom like an empty barrel. "Just hang tough, you three. And keep those slots covered against any thirty-thirty slugs. Let's go, boys."

Marsh Bailor caught up his calico pony, and the three riders swept east along the dusty road at a full gallop. Lark guessed that they had less than an hour before the bandits came down the mountain trail from Box B.

Where a jagged rock face jutted out almost to the bank of the river, the road bent, bent so sharply that the rock side was scarred by horizontal lines scraped by the big freight tandems as they struggled around the point. Beyond this bend was a cove, wooded, a good-sized creek dropping into it, a flurry of foamed water splashing from one mossy ledge to the next.

"Right here," Marsh said, reining in his pony.

Lark stood in his stirrups to survey the lightly wooded area. After a minute, he nodded, and dropped back into the saddle. He clucked to Mingus and they moved out. "They'll have good cover, and even a light wagon will have to slow down for that sharp bend."

"They'll have marksmen on the slope above. That's their usual tactic," Tetrault said. "If we could get above them . . ."

"We will. And we'll have a box seat when the ball opens," Lark said. "Marsh, if you want out, because of your family and all, just you point out where your mountain trail starts, and you hightail it."

Marsh shook his head. "Uh-uh, Mr. Lark. I ain't scairt, and I'll stick with you men. I ain't sayin' I'll throw down on Buzz or Anse, or Pike Sumter, but as fer any of the rest, I'd as soon put a thirty-thirty through 'em as spit."

"You're our man, then," Lark said approvingly.

They were two miles past the cove named by Marsh Bailor as the ambush area, when they rounded a promontory and found a similar indentation, except more shallow, the plunging creek smaller, the brush thinner. Marsh turned his pony off onto an almost invisible game trail. At the end of the cul-de-sac he halted his horse. He pointed at the slope where the trail broke out of the woodsy shade and twisted, climbing, into the broken rocks and out of sight.

"There she is," he said.

"All right for deer, but not saddle horses," Tetrault said.

"It ain't," Marsh said.

"Or even mules," Lark said, patting Mingus on the

145

shoulder. He swung down. "It's shank's mare, then. We'll make better time and less noise."

He knotted the reins to a tree limb, and slipped his Winchester from the saddle boot. He looked up the steepness of the trail and took a deep breath. "All right, boys. Let's go."

14

Pinkerton's National Detective Agency
District Office, Denver, Colorado
File 262—The Redtop Case
   Daily Report Operative J. Lark not received cov-
ering July 25 & 26, 1887, et seq. See telegram C.
Tetrault dated July 27, explaining hiatus in daily
record.

                    S. Eames, Supervisor

◄◄◄◄◄◄◄◄◄◄◄◄◄◄◄◄◄◄◄◄◄◄◄◄◄◄◄◄◄◄

Lark toiled up the steep reaches, grabbing for hand-holds, digging the heels of his boots into the resistant gravel of the slope. He reflected that he should be weary. He had been up before sunrise, had ridden thirty miles and more, and had for nights on end been getting less than a normal quota of sleep. Yet he was not tired. Instead he felt invigorated, alert, powerful, as if no test could daunt him. He recognized the high stimulation of danger, as the climax of a difficult and dangerous case neared a conclusion. And as always he pushed back into a dark niche of his mind the knowledge that death itself could come to Justin Lark before this still hot day was over.

He signaled for a breather, and they sat gratefully with their backs against a boulder. Tetrault, the horseman, was breathing harshly from this unaccustomed exercise. Marsh, inured to these altitudes and armored by the resilience of his youth, was barely breathing fast, though sweat matted the hair at his temples and gleamed in fine beads on forehead and upper lip.

Somewhere in between I come, Lark thought ruefully. When I was as young as Marsh, I would have given him a run for his money. I do have the edge on Con a little; I've done more walking lately, and I gave up those Havana seegars many a moon ago. Just the same, there's one tough old hombre. I couldn't name one man I'd sooner have siding me in a tight spot like this one.

They had climbed a considerable way up the rock face. Lark could see below them the broken canyon, the brawling waters of the Redstone, and at one brief stretch between the trees, the ribbon of dust that was the road. The treetops of the cove they had left were far below them. To his right, Lark could follow the lace of the falling creek, as the water spun into streamers and plumes of white froth, dropping from rock to rock. The air was sharp and clean, tangy with the smell of spruce and pine. Somewhere in tree or sky a bird cried the same few notes over and over. There was little breeze, but even in full sunshine the July heat was not oppressive.

A deer fly lit on the back of Lark's hand, but before it could nip a chunk of flesh he smashed the sluggish insect with a sweep of his hand. That's how Sascha Verloff means to smash me, he thought. Not surprised, really, that he's set me up for execution. I've served his purpose, or so he thinks, and now I know too much. He's a respectable adversary; he plays for keeps. He's big game, and dangerous. But this game I'll win.

A thought came to Lark then, one that hadn't occurred to him before. Perhaps his death warrant at Verloff's hands stemmed back to the lovely Sonya. He had seen that Verloff was intensely protective of his sister. He may have seen the rapport that was building between her and Lark, and decided that Lark must go sooner instead of later. I'd be a new factor for him to cope with, if Sonya were on my side, he thought. And

147

again the tantalizing mystery of the girl nagged at him —how much does she know? How much does she go along with Sascha's boundless ambition? What do I mean to her? Could she be the brains, the planner, the architect of the Verloff empire?

I'm going over thrice-plowed ground again, he told himself. Those damned suspicions—if I must be the instrument to send that lovely dark-haired girl to grave or gallows, I'll have no peace with myself forever. That promise she has shown me in mind and body is an excitement that lifts me beyond all yearning, into a hope beyond all price. If it ends in ashes . . .

He thought of Rimi then, proud uncomplicated Rimi, a girl he loved in a gentle way and always would love. He admired her pluck, and her clean conscience, and her intelligence. But for him she held none of the breathless excitement of Sonya Verloff. Moreover, there was Con Tetrault. He glanced at his companion, calm of visage and no doubt of soul, a solid and dependable man. The way Con had touched Rimi, the hand held longer than need be, the eyes following her movements, had not escaped Lark. You should be jealous, Justin, he thought. But he knew he was not, and for Rimi and for Con he could feel only happiness.

Lark drew a deep breath and levered himself to his feet. "Got your wind back? Let's move it, then."

They topped the ridge half an hour later and started down the west slope. There was a well-defined game trail which wound across bare slopes and through scrub timber. Between the trees it was pleasantly cool, but in the open the sun at zenith scorched from the shale, and the heat hung as oppressive as an oven. Lark spat cotton and wished they had brought a canteen of water. Instead, for moisture he pulled long joints of grass and chewed the tender stalk ends.

They were moving downhill through a thin grove of scraggly pine when Tetrault hissed, "Down! There they are!"

They hunkered down under cover of the evergreens, peering through the lacy branches, with a good view of the far side of the valley. That side was more open and less timbered, yet marked by a trail

148

similar to the one they had been following. They could see the path looping along the steep face, always dropping, toward the timbered cove, no doubt for the water available at the bottom. It was a track engineered by instinct and worn into being by the sharp hooves of elk and deer. It was a path to be negotiated with care by horse or mule, heavier and less sure-footed.

Lark counted the riders as they inched along the steep track. Four—six—nine—twelve—thirteen. Lark shook his head. They must have dragooned every hardcase in the whole county for this job. He stared across the valley, eyes narrowed, wishing he had field glasses. But in this clear air, this brilliant sunlight, even small details could be made out. Lark recognized Anse Bailor, and Buzz, and Pike Sumter. My executioners, he thought grimly. And ah, yes, there at the rear of the column was Sascha Verloff, elegantly attired, as unperturbed as if this were a mere hunting party. Which of course it is, Lark thought, but for the most dangerous game of all—man.

He heard a quick intake of breath by Marsh, beside him. The boy said, "Hey, Mr. Lark, right back of Anse and Buzz, you see them three?"

"Strangers to me, son," Lark admitted.

"That's Pete Looby, by God, and two of his deputies! The high sheriff of Antelope County! Ain't that somethin'?"

"You didn't know Looby was tied in with the Red-tops?"

"Uh-uh. Buzz was always shooting off his mouth about the law couldn't touch him or Anse or Lippy, but he never said why. I guess we got the answer."

"Marsh, there's nothing rottener than a crooked lawman," Lark said. No wonder murder ran rampant; no wonder Rod Starbolt could hold up the stagecoach in utter impunity. And rage rose in Lark until his clenched hand shook with it. Only with a deliberate effort did he regain his self-control.

"See that rock outcrop below, Con?" he asked. "Let's work our way down there. Looks like it will be as good as a box seat at the opera house."

"And with a clear range of fire," Tetrault added.

They were rounding a huge boulder, almost to their goal, when Lark gave Marsh a quick thrust back behind the rock. Con stopped too, watching, listening. There was the sound of voices, and the scrape of boot soles on the rocks. Two men came over the hump from below, and stopped at the flat of the same promontory Lark and his men had been aiming for. They were talking in normal tones, careless of danger, cocksure there was no one else in the area. No wonder, Lark thought, so many desperadoes end in prison or on the gallows. They haven't got the brains to smell danger, or the ambition to watch for it. Seems like the damn fools have an itch to get themselves caught.

The two newcomers stood in the tree shade, as if reluctant to venture once more into the fierce blaze of sun. One of them, Lark recognized, was a Rail Fence puncher. The other was one of the two deputies Marsh had pointed out.

"C'mon, Tex," the deputy said. "We gotta get out there. The boss will be checkin' to see if we're in position."

"T'ell with the furriner," the puncher said. "He kilt Rod Starbolt like a shoat in a butcher shop." He pulled a flask from his pocket. "Here, take a swig. It'll keep our brains from fryin' out in them rocks. Hey, forget what I said about Verloff. I didn't mean nothin'."

"I know, I know," the deputy said, tipping the bottle. When he lowered it he gave a loud burp of satisfaction.

Lark rose upright, with a motion of his head to Con Tetrault. His partner nodded, and came erect. In ten quick steps they covered the distance to the two men, steps almost silent on the decayed duff under the trees. Any sound came too late to warn the two men.

There was an arm around each throat, a crushing pressure on the windpipe. The only noise was the scuff of feet, and a strangled grunt. The rifles fell, the revolvers were plucked from holsters and tossed out of reach.

"You make a sound and you're dead!" Lark hissed. He nudged his man with the muzzle of his pistol. The man's shoulders slumped. With a quick twist, Lark brought the man's arms behind the back, and there was a crisp click of handcuffs. He lifted the man's neckerchief and jammed it cruelly tight into the man's mouth, tying it in a hard knot behind the head. Roughly, he thrust the man toward the uphill trail.

He saw Tetrault handcuff the other man and thrust him to his feet. They herded the two up the trail and behind the boulder. Marsh Bailor followed, with the guns he had gathered up. There was a look of wondering admiration on his young face, a tribute to the speed and efficiency of the bandits' subjection.

They secured the feet of the men, and dragged them to a sitting position back of the rock. Lark said, "Marsh, I want you to stay right here and guard these two. Don't untie them for any reason—if they say they have to go, let 'em wet their pants. Any false moves, shoot 'em in the leg, then the other leg. Don't take the gags out of their mouths. Understand?"

"Yes, sir, Mr. Lark!" Marsh said, and waved the big hogleg Colt at the prisoners. Lark slapped him on the shoulder in approval. Then he and Tetrault hurried toward the jutting rock.

They peered over the edge. There was a small group of men gathered in the open glade just off the road, all of them staring up at the rock. Lark let the top of his head show, and waved Tex's Stetson in a circle. Then he dropped back out of sight, behind the parapet.

"They bought it," Tetrault said, grinning. "They've scattered. Two of 'em gone across the cove to the far wall."

"Same play," Lark said. "I was in one of 'em, remember? Now the waiting starts."

"And that's the hellishing worst part of all," Tetrault grumbled. He made himself comfortable, resting his rifle in a notch of the rock. He thumbed the hammer to full cock. "You make it about two hundred yards? To the road, I mean?"

"Or a hair over," Lark said, adjusting the rear sight of his rifle. He settled down to wait, his lean body relaxed. But his mind was racing, scanning the possibilities and the probabilities of the situation. He hoped that all holes were plugged. Yet from long experience, he knew that operas like this were played by ear. There is action and reaction, not always what a man might expect. Wish I had my guitar up here, he thought, and smiled sardonically as he imagined the jolt the men below would get if the strains of "The Hangman's Song" came floating down from the heights.

He glanced at the sun. Noon, he thought, and checked it by his watch. Since Rankine had not yet showed, it meant he was following orders to the letter. Lark could see that the unexpected delay was plucking at the nerves of the Redtops. One man donned his red mask and began to untie his horse, evidently intending to ride west to locate the wagon. With a show of anger, the man Marsh had pointed out as Pete Looby, the sheriff, restrained the would-be rider with some force. The man retired his mount and dropped back into the brush. All was quiet.

Thirteen of the enemy, and three friends, all in the narrow confines of this cove, Lark thought. Hardly anything to show it, a battered hat here, a protruding boot there. The sun seared from a flawless sky, the river surged its relentless way toward Starr Valley, the birds sang, the squirrels chattered among the branches. And this peaceful scene would soon erupt in violence and death, Lark thought. A play which I have written: the cues are mine, I move the actors from place to place upon this stage, and take a leading role myself. Neither as actor or playwright can I have much effect; the play must run its course.

"They're coming," Con Tetrault said softly. "The guard at the bend must hear the wagon."

Lark dropped his hat beside him and raised his head cautiously to look over the rim of rock. He saw the two men at the point of rock edge back from the road. One of them fumbled a red mask over his head, the other either lacked the knitted mask or disdained to use it. In a silence broken only by the soft susurrus of the breeze, Lark heard the sound of hoofbeats and the crunch of wagon wheels. A rider came around the point of rock—Art Rankine. Lark frowned. Trust the marshal to accept the more dangerous post, leaving Collins to protect the rear. Rankine rode carelessly, as if not noting his surroundings.

The wagon turned the bend, the horses moving smartly. On the seat Raghead Willie sat erect, shadowed

152

by the canopy, as authentic as a teamster of flesh and blood. Rankine rode ahead, now past the edge of trees, now halfway across the cove. The wagon came into the open space. Then, with a shock, Lark's memory swept back to that other holdup, a month ago. By God, I've got a role in this, a key role! He dropped the bead of the front sight of his rifle into the notch of the rear sight, took a deep breath. He squeezed the trigger and shot Raghead Willie squarely through his raveled cotton heart.

The team reared, snorting, and came to a stop. Now other guns opened up, in a veritable storm of fire. But at the crack of Lark's shot, Rankine had struck spurs to his horse, and head bent low, raced past the trees and into the next bend, unscathed.

Kleberg must have loosened Raghead Willie's clamps from the inside, for the dummy toppled realistically down to the footboard and lay quiescent. Now Verloff's men came running out of the brush, toward the wagon. They fired back down the road at Collins, but he ducked safely around the point of rock. Two others ran east after Rankine, but his rifle slammed and one of the men spun into the dust, as limp as a bundle of old sacking. The other man dove aside into the sheltering brush.

Lark heard Verloff roar, "Get this damned wagon open, you men! We haven't got all day!"

Warily, the circle of men closed in on the wagon which stood strangely silent behind its uneasy team. A man tried the rear doors, then picked up a rock and started hammering at the fastening, by the sound of it. Ineffectively, it seemed, for Sascha Verloff came hurrying around the wagon. Standing at an angle to avoid a ricochet, he pumped five rifle bullets into the offending lock. And then all hell broke loose.

The slots in the steel-plated wagon body flipped open, and the riflemen inside poured fire at the circle of bandits. Men dropped, or leaped for cover, or ran. Lark clicked his sight up a notch and dropped the Redtop at the far bend. His second shot missed the other rear outpost as he tumbled into the safety of a boulder field. Tetrault too was firing, slowly, with deliberate aim.

The firing slowed. He could see three limp figures near the wagon, one on the road to the east, and the guard at the bend. Five, plus two captives here on the rock slope. He smiled in grim satisfaction. In the first flurry, Verloff's army had been reduced by half. It was time to put pressure on the rest of it.

He said, "Con, you cover me. I'm going down there." He ran, crouched low, down the steep trail toward the road and the river. He paused, panting in the steamy heat of a patch of thick brush at the bottom. A movement in the leafy greenery to his right and he wheeled, rifle poised. He called softly, "That you, Art?"

Rankine said, "Yeah. Had a couple of close ones, but none with my name on it. Any of ours hurt, Justin?"

"Just Raghead Willie. I think he's dead," Lark said, as he eased out of the brush to stand beside Rankine. "Seven of theirs down. We've got 'em just about outgunned."

"And time is on our side," Rankine said. "Verloff's with 'em? He's got to make a move soon."

"He will. But he's got the law on his side, Art. Pete Looby and two deputies, if you can believe that."

"The hell!" Rankine exclaimed, and swore softly and bitterly. "No wonder the Redtops were so bold. Justin, these hellions just about had the whole country the way they wanted it."

"So this has got to be the end for them," Lark said. "So let's finish it. Con's above, Ted's forted up on the far side. You and I will move in from behind them, and drive them toward the firepower of the boys in the wagon."

As noiselessly as they could, the two men pushed through the brush and stepped into the shallow waters of the creek. The chill of the swift water felt good at first, then their legs and feet grew numb. Rankine stepped into a hole and went hip-deep, and only Lark's quick grab kept the marshal from going under. They slipped and stumbled on the slimy stones until Lark guessed they were beyond the perimeter of the bandits. He jerked a thumb at Rankine, and the two

154

men came over the low bank and stood alert in a clump of alder, listening. Nothing.

Lark whispered. "Art, keep within a few feet of me. We'll work toward the wagon and see if we flush anyone out."

A hundred feet farther, and Rankine's hand went up. Ahead, a man was crouched by a tree, his back to them. Lark held his rifle ready, and Rankine, reaching down, picked up a dry stick. He snapped it with a loud crack. The man swiveled around, his mouth dropping open in surprise. Anse Bailor.

"You're covered, Bailor," Lark said quietly. "Drop the gun."

But Bailor's reaction was the feral defiance of a trapped weasel. He spun toward them, his hand coming around. He managed to trigger one shot, close enough to brush Rankine's hat, before Lark killed him with a single shot through the head. Bailor plunged into the forest duff and lay still. Lark stared at the body a moment, feeling no remorse, remembering Lolly.

The two eased away to better cover as a drumfire of bullets swept the place where they had been. Lark heard Rankine grunt. "You hit, Art?"

"Leg graze," Rankine said, but the clenched sound of the marshal's voice told Lark the wound was painful. "I'll make it. Let's keep moving."

Ahead there was a rattle of firing. A high shrill cry keened from the roadside. Four left, Lark counted. We're cutting 'em down to size.

Ahead, there came the tremendous crash of an explosion, the impact jarring Lark and Rankine, even among the trees. They've blown up the wagon! Lark thought in panic. What did it do to my three men, cooped up in that steel box? If they're hurt or killed, by God, I'll make Verloff pay . . . Heedless of enemy fire, he jammed his way through the brush to the road, Rankine limping behind him. He stood in the open, rifle ready.

The wagon stood quiet, still on four wheels, but with some of its exterior canvas blown away. One of the horses was down, struggling in the harness, the other standing terrified, eyes bulging and red-rimmed.

155

Just off the road, near the wagon, lay what had once been a man, but was now only a shapeless mass of ragged flesh and charred clothing. Only its head had been strangely untouched, and Lark recognized it—Buzz Bailor. Four men left, three? Verloff, Looby, who else? Would Verloff give up now, or would he run?

Lark's answer came quickly. Seldom in his dangerous career did he underestimate an opponent, but he had now. From the Gap side came a thunder of racing hoofs. Lark heard Collins's rifle fire once, twice, and a flurry of pistol fire in return. Six riders came sweeping toward the wagon.

Lark yelled, "Val! Fred! Robbie! More visitors, coming in from the west. Watch it!" And he and Rankine jumped back into the cover of the brush. From its leafy screen Lark saw another rider coming, spurring hard, bent low over the neck of the horse. Then the wave of riders hit the wagon, firing point-blank as the steel slots blazed with return fire.

Horses went down, men went down. Lark and Rankine were firing as fast as they could work the levers of their repeaters. Lark's hammer clicked on an empty chamber, and he dropped the rifle, pulled his pistol from the holster. Three of the newcomers were still in action, a fourth, unhorsed, was firing from the road. Lark recognized them—Rail Fence riders, Verloff's own picked gunmen. He fired at one, Jules the footman, his high silk topper traded for a battered Stetson and a deadly forty-five. Jules, hit, threw up his arms and plunged from his horse, skidding like a thrown bundle in the dust of the road.

The fire from inside the armored wagon was too intense for even these desperate men to face. They broke, and rode back, away from the wagon, toward the seventh rider, who was calming a horse made nervous by the crash of firing. Lark stared—that straight back, the long black hair streaming away from the face—my God, it's Sonya! What crazy idea has brought her here?

From the depths of the brush charged four mounted men, one with a white rag of bandage around his head in lieu of a hat. They joined the two new riders who remained. Lark recognized two, Pete Looby, and of

156

course, Sascha Verloff. As they broke from the brush, Sonya urged her horse toward them. She raised her hand to stop them.

Lark, ignoring possible fire, moved into the clear space of the road. The knot of riders seemed to be having an argument. Verloff edged his powerful horse ahead, forcing Sonya's mount back and back, across the road. As he turned his horse west, she spurred her own mount into the press of riders. And from someone's hand fire lanced at her. Not Verloff's.

The girl's horse reared, screaming. It went high, forefeet pawing the air, then the horse pinwheeled on the narrow road and lurched over the river bank into the turbulent waters of the Redstone. Verloff's mount drove forward. Then at the very brink, Lark saw Verloff twist the horse's head around, and with the other riders behind him, race west around the sharp bend of rock and out of sight.

"Art, get the boys out of that wagon!" Lark yelled, and ran toward the river, jerking the buckle of his cartridge belt loose as he ran. If the horse fell on her she's done, he thought frantically. He stopped at the edge of the current, shading his eyes with a palm against the glare of sun on water. Nothing—nothing but the swirl of froth and foam, the slide and swoop of the rapids, the splash of the racing current against the boulders.

Then he saw it sweeping toward him—the flash of a white face, the black hair streaming away from it. It went under, but he had seen enough. He launched his body into the water. Mauled by the driving current, he felt cloth under his hand, but it tore away. Desperately he hooked out a hand again, caught leather, the belt of the man's trousers the girl had donned for this desperate ride. The slash of the current drove him against a boulder and he felt bone go, but he kept his body between Sonya and the cruel rock. Then the very viciousness of the cascade hurled them up into the shallows. Lark came to his knees, then his feet. With the girl in his arms he staggered to the safety of the bank.

He laid her head down on the river bank, and began pressing rhythmically on her back with one hand, for the other dangled useless at his side. As Rankine and Val Kleberg hurried up, the girl coughed, spewed water, coughed again. She tried to sit up. Her dark eyes came open, focused. "Justin, eet is you!" she cried, and was caught in another spasm of coughing. When it was over she stood up, leaning against Lark, the color coming back into her face. "Sascha, my brother—he say you are dead!" She fumbled at the man's shirt whe wore, trying to close the torn cloth over the lovely contours of her bosom.

"I'm battered but alive," Lark said, trying to smile. "But Sonya, why are you here? Who attacked you?"

The tears welled in those great dark eyes. "Because I am so stupid, I should be punished. Not until now do I know what Sascha ees doing. No, zat ees not right—not until now do I let myself believe w'at I know he ees doing. I am like ze lamb led to ze slaughter, Justin. I am just as guilty as my brother, for zere is no place in zis worl' for anyone so stupid as me. Only when I learn zat you are to be killed, do my eyes come open. Zen I begin to see things as zey are. And I try to stop it, and I try to save your life, and zey shoot at me and hit my horse, and you should in zat river have let me drown!"

15

Pinkerton's National Detective Agency
District Office, Denver, Colorado
File 262—The Redtop Case
    No Entry This Date—J. Lark, Operative
        (Signed) S. Eames, Supervisor

◄◄◄◄◄◄◄◄◄◄◄◄◄◄◄◄◄◄◄◄◄◄◄◄◄◄◄◄◄

The girl stood for a long minute, her face buried in the wet fabric of Lark's shirt. Then, her control regained, she raised her head. Pulling away from Lark's supporting arm, she took both hands and wrung the water from her long tresses, careless of the white flesh revealed by her torn clothing. She looked at Lark's men, Rankine with the long red-black stain of blood down his pants leg, Val Kleberg with head bandaged for a wound from a flying splinter, Ted Collins, face pale, holding tight to a shoulder sodden with blood. Nordstrom and Loucks were unhurt, but they rubbed ears partly deafened from the dynamite explosion set off so close to them. Con Tetrault and Marsh Bailor, herding their prisoners before them, were the only ones who showed no scars of battle.

"Sonya, I've got to have answers," Lark said. "How much did you know about——" He swept an arm toward the scene of carnage. "——about this, about your brother."

Her eyes were sad. "I am stupid, Justin, but more, I am selfish. I suspect all zees money, I make myself believe Sascha when he say eet is investments, from our friends, and our kin in Poznan, he buy ze business, ze lands for them. I *want* to believe him, Justin; I am afraid of ze truth zat is far in my mind. Only today eet come out so I mus' listen, I learn that Sascha is ze boss—ze *directeur* of ze whole thing, he have kill people, he have robbed, and today he kill and rob once again. So I mus' try to stop it."

"So you dress like a boy, ride here hell-bent to stop it, only to find it is all over?" There was a tinge of irony in Lark's words. "Sonya, I'd like to believe you. But I find it hard. How could you learn this today? And today only?"

"Ze woman Amy, Rod Starbolt's woman. She tell Sascha zat Starbolt do not tell her any thing. But he do. She is going to leave for Magma, I help her, give her money. Because I show pity for Starbolt, because I play sad violin for his burial, this morning, before she go, she tell me everything, ze Redtops, ze murders, even ze plan to rob ze treasure wagon today. And she make me understand, though I do not want to understand, zat my Sascha, he ees ze key man to everything. And she say Tex, who ees mad at my brother, he tell her you are Pinkerton man, and you weel be killed first thing. Justin, I could not—I could

159

not let zat happen. Eet would be mos' terrible thing in my life."

Her story is convincing, Lark thought. Maybe, like Sonya, I want to be convinced. I see a few holes in it, but . . .

"Just now, why did Sascha shoot at you?" he asked.

"Not Sascha, zat Pete Looby, ze sheriff. When Sascha say you have been shot, I go wild wiz anger. I try to grab gun from Looby's holster so I can shoot Sascha, shoot my own brother. Looby push me aside, he say, 'You crazy woman!' and he shoot then my horse, and we fall in river. And Sascha, he jus' ride away!"

"He just rode away," Lark said gently, and his good arm tightened around her shoulders, the white shoulders shining through the torn shirt in the bald sunlight. "He's heading for Rail Fence, I'd bet, to pick up whatever stake he can lay his hands on, then he'll head for Canada. We've got to pick him up."

"Zis failure—Justin, my brother weel be a broken man," she said. "Cannot you just let him go?"

"He has too many dead men to answer for," Lark said harshly. He nodded toward the limp figures stretched along the dusty road, the flies drifting around them in clouds already. "If he goes free, he'll recover his pride and his conceit, and start building empires again. I know such men, Sonya. He will be content only when he is at the top of the heap. And he will climb there on the dead bodies of better men."

Lark's men were looking to him for directions, but when they saw the depths of his concern with Sonya, they drifted to Tetrault, who started them on the grisly chore of the cleanup. Marsh Bailor stopped, statue-still, when he saw the torn body of his brother Buzz, smashed when Tetrault's bullet had caught Buzz just as he lit the fuse of the dynamite bomb. The boy retched violently, holding tight to the wheel of the wagon. Then he took off his jacket and covered his brother's dead face.

Lark and Sonya, lost in their own agonies, stood apart on the river bank. She looked up at Lark now, her fine eyes starred with tears. "I know you are right, Justin. But ze blood runs thick and red in ze Polish

160

family. When Sascha was young man and I was small child, he was my big brother and I adore him. Zen he was fine man, simple, sweet. Zen by bribery and treachery, our estate ees taken from us, our land, all zat we own. My father, he is crushed, he take his own life. My brother, he turn bitter. He come to America to make fortune to show ze worl', he will be tough and cruel too. When I come with him to Montana, I think he has gotten over that, but when I see him building great fortune in land, in cattle, I am suspec' him, zat he ees not my kind brother any more. So now it all end like this, in blood and flies and dead men in ze road . . ." She moved her hand in a gesture of helplessness.

"You'll get over it, Sonya dear. You'll have to," Lark said. "I'll help you pick up what pieces may be left. But now I'm going to take you to the Gap. Rimi will help you, take care of you, until everything is over." She tried to smile but could not.

Tetrault said, "We've cleaned up the worst of it. I told Val to stay until the U.S. marshals get here. The kid's bringing horses. But you're not going to ride, Justin." He touched Lark's shoulder and at the grate of bone Lark almost screamed. "You've got a busted collarbone at the very least, and likely some cracked ribs."

He climbed into the wagon and slashed at the inert form of Raghead Willie. Triumphantly he pulled out a large piece of white cloth. "One of Rimi's old petticoats," he said. "I remembered just where we stuffed it when we were making the dummy."

With the quick expertise of the man who was used to patching field injuries, he fashioned a sling for Lark's damaged arm, and bound the bent arm close to the body. Lark groaned now and then during the operation, but when Tetrault was through the shoulder did not pain him as fiercely, and Lark could move more easily. "If you won't let me ride, I'll drive the team," he told Tetrault. "Art, get your sore leg into the wagon, and keep an eye on Ted. He looks feverish." With an effort he climbed up on the wagon seat. Tetrault picked Sonya up in his arms and set her effortlessly on the seat beside Lark.

But it was Sonya who freed the reins from the steel slot. Holding them, she stepped past Lark to the driver's side of the seat. "I weel handle ze team. Are ze horses all right?"

"They'll make it," Tetrault said, stroking the velvet noses of the team. "Buck got scared when the dynamite went off, got tangled in the harness, but he's all right now."

"Horse wasn't the only one scared when that thing went off," Loucks said. "I thought the end of the world had come. It about busted our eardrums. C'mon, Robbie, let's find ourselves a couple of horses. There's plenty whose riders won't need 'em any more."

Although Lark had urged his men to move fast, the riders did not get very far ahead of the wagon. There was always the chance of Verloff, in his desperation, staging a last ditch attempt at a second ambush. He watched Sonya handle the tired team with expert hands. She avoided the larger rocks when she could, in deference to the wounded men, who were settled on the sacking and the dismantled stuffing of Raghead Willie. But in spite of her care she and Lark would hear a groan now and then when the wagon dropped into one of the deeper thank-you-ma'ams.

Lark was coming out of the effects of shock and battle haze. His mind was alert again, and he had a thousand questions he wanted to ask this girl beside him. It would require her answers to tie up the loose ends of this business, so Pinkerton File 262, The Redtop Case, could be stamped CLOSED. The dead men would be buried, the stolen wealth returned as far as possible to the rightful owners, and the guilty tried and punished. Those hurt in soul or body must begin to heal as best they could. That was the inexorable character of Lark's dangerous profession.

He admitted he had broken the primary rule of Allan Pinkerton: "Never get emotionally involved with any person in your case, whether client or suspect." He had become involved with Rimi Woodford, which could be mended, and with Sonya Verloff, which might be irretrievable. That was why he hesitated to question Sonya. The suspicion that twisted in his vitals like a hot knife had not been allayed. If she is lying,

162

if she is guilty—Lark scowled at the thought. Here's Justin Lark, he thought, the cold-blooded manhunter, the impartial seeker of justice, fallen in love with a woman who might be guilty of heartless and monstrous crimes. And if I find it true, God help me, all my life is changed.

They were little more than a mile from the Gap when Sonya said softly, "Justin, you must hate me. If I had been truthful with you, if I had told to you my suspicions of Sascha, it may be much wicked things would be avoided. But I am coward."

"I'm not sure I wouldn't have done things the same way," Lark said. "Blood is thicker than water, and that's the truth."

"Yet too many time eet is just ze excuse," she said, and there was bitterness in her voice. "Justin, I like ze fine house, ze music, ze blood horses. I do not open ze eyes wide, for fear I disturb these nice things I haff. I say nossing, and now men have died because I kept silent, and women will weep. I keep ze nice house, play ze piano and violin, plan ze good meals, pick ze right wine, and keep ze mouth and ze eyes shut. Justin, I am a person ver' weak, I think. Here in ze West, ze cowboy he would call me ze damn fool."

"Blaming yourself isn't the answer, my dear," Lark said. "What's over is done. We've got to push it aside and start over. Tell me you'll do that."

She looked at him, her penance unallayed, the tears still tangled in her thick lashes. On impulse he leaned over and kissed her, feeling those soft lips respond under his. When at last they broke apart, she murmured, "Oh, Justin, Justin, you are still believing in me!"

They swept around the final turn and broke out of Stoneman's Gap. Ahead of them was the inn, gleaming white in the harsh sunlight. But ranged around the building were armed men, a small army, their attention evidently concentrated on the inn building. Sonya turned the team into the loop of the driveway and Ted Powell, the rancher, stepped out, hand upraised. Sonya pulled the weary team to a halt.

"What in God's name is up, Ted?" Lark demanded.

"Verloff. He's holed up inside with three of his

163

men. He's holding Rimi and Goldie as hostages. We don't know what to do about it, except to keep them pinned down." The rancher's voice was grim and worried. "Sorry, Miss Verloff," he added.

"Give it to me straight, Ted. What happened?"

"Before he rode away, Marsh Bailor told his sister Lolly what he had learned from Buzz the night before. Lolly was afraid to tell you men, for fear of what you might do to Marsh. But after you had gone into the canyon, she told Miss Rimi. Rimi forted up in the place and sent Lolly to my place for help, and Phil to Anchor. We threw together a crew and got here just as Verloff and his men came boiling out of the Gap, hellbent for election. They threw lead at us and we shot back. We downed some of 'em, but Verloff and a couple others stormed the inn and overpowered Rimi. I don't think they hurt her or Goldie, but they say they'll kill them if we don't clear the road for 'em and let them go free. I'm glad you're here to take over. It's got me stumped."

"You did fine, just fine, Ted," Lark said. He got awkwardly down from the wagon and stood staring at the inn. Sonya wrapped the reins around the whipstock and jumped down with sure grace. She stood beside Lark, forgetful of her ragged attire, her shoulder touching his. Her lips pursed, she too stared at the building.

"They give you a deadline, Ted?" Lark asked.

"An hour. There's maybe fifteen minutes left of it."

Lark heard Sonya's quick intake of breath. "Oh, no, zey cannot hurt Rimi, zey cannot do zat. Justin, I mus' talk to Sascha. I will make him let zem go."

He touched her pale cheek. "Kid, you know what happened to you back there in the canyon. Sascha rode off and left you to drown. Would he do any more for you now?"

"He mus' listen to me, Justin; he mus'. If he has his men hurt me, keel me, I do not care. If anything happen to Rimi, I do not want to live, I theenk. Justin, let me go."

Lark looked at Powell, at Con Tetrault, at Art Rankine. Tetrault's face was gray under the tan. He said,

164

"Justin, if that devil hurts Rimi I'll storm the place and tear him apart with my bare hands. I'll . . ."

"Hold it, Con," Lark said harshly. "You're not helping things any. Sonya wants to go in and talk him into surrendering."

"He'll never do it, never," Tetrault said. "But if she's got the guts to try it, let her go. Does she know she may get hurt or killed?"

"I do," Sonya answered for herself. "But I want to try."

Lark's reluctance held him like a vise, but he nodded to Ted Powell. "A shootout's no good, just means more people killed. Maybe the girls, too. Ted, they know your voice. Tell 'em that Sonya is coming in."

Though he knew there were guns trained on the door, the rancher went up the steps without flinching. Cupping his hands around his mouth, he called through the screen door in a stentorian voice, "Verloff, hold your fire! Your sister Sonya is coming in to talk to you."

The rejoinder from inside was muffled. But even if it were negative, Sonya was already up the steps with that graceful quickness of hers, and pulling open the screen door. She stepped inside and the door slammed shut behind her. There was silence.

The minutes dragged on, longer and thinner, and more taut. Lark chewed on the fingernails of his good hand, the pain in shoulder and back nagging at him, but a pain inconsequential to the turmoil anguishing his mind. Beside him Con Tetrault leaned toward the door as tense as a hunting dog straining toward a treed cougar. His hand was tight on the checkered stock of the pistol at his hip.

Quick steps came echoing across the hardwood floor. The screen opened. Sonya stepped out, and came hurrying across the porch and down the steps. There was a shaky small smile on her pale face. "Eet ees all right," she said. "Sascha, he ees letting them go." Tetrault made a move toward the steps, but she stopped him. "Wait, Mr. Tetrault. Please wait."

So they stood in that awesome quiet, the harsh heat of the afternoon blazing down, not conscious of the discomfort, waiting. Now the screen door opened and

165

a man came out, hands held high and empty. Another man and another, in surrender. The third man wore a star gleaming on his vest. Lark felt a spurt of anger—Pete Looby, the sheriff, and the son-of-a-bitch has the audacity to wear the badge of honest office on his chest!

Ted Powell and Art Rankine and the rest gathered the three in quickly, frisked them for armaments, and led them away. At the foot of the steps, the waiting grew tense again. Then the screen opened again, and Rimi and Goldie came rushing across the porch and down the steps. Rimi's glance flitted across Lark. It was when she saw Tetrault that she smiled. His arm went around her. "Thank God, kitten," he said. "Thank God you're safe."

She was holding a folded paper. She handed it to Sonya. But oddly, the Polish girl did not look at it. She stood staring at the building, her eyes blank. Powell put a foot on the step, but Sonya said with sharp decisiveness, "Wait."

Then, from inside the building came the muffled slam of a single shot. Sonya Verloff buried her face in her hands. She said in a tortured voice, "Now—now you may go in."

The body of Sascha Verloff was slumped over the desk in Rimi's little office back of the hotel counter, the revolver still in his fingers. His face was peaceful, and the odor of burnt cloth where the powder had singed the shirt above his heart was hardly noticeable. Sonya had known her brother with sure instinct— prison or the gallows could not be fitting ends for a Verloff, and she must have convinced him that all other roads were closed to him. So the mystique of the true gentleman, which he had spent all his life building up, had been proven to be real. If he could not live longer like a gentleman, he could die like one. And so he had.

Lark turned on his heel and went out. He came down the steps, and as Sonya looked at him, he nodded. And in the passing of an instant, her disciplined reserve shattered, and she was just a girl crushed by the loss of a beloved brother. She came into the circle of Lark's free arm, and he held her tight against his chest. The convulsive sobbing, and the bitter tears brought her a measure of relief from shock, but they flowed on in regret and penitence.

He looked down at the sleek dark hair of that bowed head, and was caught in the tempest of his own pity, and compassion, and—he admitted to it at last—love.

16

27 JULY 1887
MANTOUL, M.T.
CABLE — SUSANEAMES
DENVER, COLORADO

OPERATION SUCCESSFUL STOP REDTOP GANG BROKEN AND DISPERSED STOP CLOSE FILE TWO SIX STOP YOUR NEPHEW JUSTIN HURT BUT NOT SERIOUSLY STOP WILL COME TO DENVER ABOUT AUGUST SEVEN WITH FULL REPORT STOP TELL CLIENTS WILL BE ABLE TO MAKE RESTITUTION OF LARGE PART OF STOLEN FUNDS ON VOLUNTARY BASIS THOUGH SOME TIME MAY BE RE-QUIRED TO COMPLETE NEEDED REAL ESTATE TRANS-FERS AND SALES STOP TEMPORARY OPERATIVE ART RANKINE HAS BEEN APPOINTED SHERIFF OF ANTE-LOPE COUNTY AND WILL BE AVAILABLE TO COM-PLETE CASE STOP

OPERATIVE LARK WILL BRING FEMALE OPERATIVE UNCLE ALLAN HAS WANTED YOU TO EMPLOY TO DENVER WITH HIM STOP VERY TALENTED, SPEAKS FOUR LANGUAGES AND HAS COURAGE OF A SHE-BEAR WITH CUBS, PLAYS VIOLIN LIKE ANGEL AND WILL BE GREAT ASSET TO AGENCY AND TO J. LARK STOP HE ASKS THAT YOU TRY TO LOCATE PRIEST WHO SPEAKS FLUENT POLISH TO BE READY WHEN HE REACHES DENVER STOP IMPORTANT STOP

OPERATIVE TETRAULT HEREBY SUBMITS RESIGNA-TION FROM AGENCY AS OF AUGUST ONE TO TAKE

POSITION AS ASSISTANT MANAGER STONEMAN'S INN, STONEMAN'S GAP, M.T. STOP REGRET SHORT NOTICE BUT OPPORTUNITY TOO GOOD TO PASS UP STOP END MESSAGE

OPERATIVE CONRAD TETRAULT

168

WESTERNS
from
BB
BALLANTINE BOOKS

BUFFALO HUNT
Mel Marshall
$.95

TEMPORARY DUTY
Wade Everett
$.95

GUT SHOT
Lee Leighton
$.95

▼ Available at your local bookstore or mail the coupon below ▼

BB 28/75

MORE DOUBLE **B** WESTERNS
from
BB
BALLANTINE BOOKS

THE FORBIDDEN LAND
Hunter Ingram   **$.95**

BUGLE AND SPUR
Brian Garfield   **$.95**

FORT APACHE
Hunter Ingram   **$.95**

BIG UGLY
Lee Leighton   **$.95**
